RT Books Presents:
The Haunted West

Volume Two

Virginia Henley

Eileen Dreyer

Carole Nelson Douglas

Erin McCarthy

Kathy Love

Elle J. Rossi

Deborah Grahl

Mathew Kaufman

Crystal Perkins

Leah Snow

Featuring a bonus story from RT BookLovers 2018 contest winner

J. Piper Lee

Jen — Thanks for the support and cheerleading! Enjoy!

13Thirty Books
Print and Digital Editions
Copyright 2018

Discover new and exciting works by 13Thirty Books at
www.13thirtybooks.com

Print and Digital Edition, License Notes

DEDICATION

Thank you RT for making the romance industry what it is today. RT is truly the luminary of the industry.

Thank you Kathryn, Carol, Ken, Jo Carol, Kate, and all the RT staff for your perseverance, dedication, guidance, and ingenuity, which knows no bounds.

CONTENTS

FOREWORD

Diana Gabaldon

I grew up in the West and–aside from a brief and horrible eighteen months on the east coast (major culture shock)–have always lived here. My old family home is in Flagstaff, at the foot of an extinct volcano that is a sacred mountain to at least thirteen local Native American tribes, including the Hopi and the Navajo (to whom it 's Dook 'o 'oosłííd, the sacred mountain of the west, built with pieces of abalone shell brought from the Third World).

Out beyond the mountains, on the high desert near Sunset Crater, are the ruins of Wupatki and Wukoki, built more than a thousand years ago by people we call the Sinagua or Anasazi, because they are lost, along with their names. I've sat (a long time ago, lest the National Park Service become Concerned…) on a wall at Wupatki by the light of a full moon and listened to the earth breathe, through blowholes from the caves below. I mean, you want to talk haunted?

And then to the south, among the low deserts and their mountains and mirages, we have the stories of lost miners, cowboys and desperate gun-slingers: think the OK Corral, Wyatt Earp and Doc Holiday, Boot Hill and Tombstone (one of my grandfathers was at one time editor of *The Tombstone Epitaph*, the town 's newspaper, which I thought was pretty neat). There's even an official ghost-town–Jerome, in the Mingus Mountains, a (mostly) abandoned mining town–though there are a lot of less-known places in the

Southwest where people have once lived… and maybe still do, though their earthly traces have vanished.

And that's just Arizona.

What I mean is, you could hardly find more fertile ground than the West, if what you want is a peek through the veil between this world and… others.

The stories in this book are a fascinating array of paranormal suspense, romance, and mystery, where parted lovers find each other on the other side of death and the spirits of dead killers still roam among the living. If love never dies… does evil?

In a long life of walking battlefields and ferreting through the past, I've often sensed Things–everyone does, I think. Nobody visits Culloden without feeling the presence of its dead. I've been in a lot of very old places, from Scotland to the Sonoran desert, and if you sit still and listen, you definitely get Echoes. But in terms of specific, individual, *personal* ghosts… I've met only three. I mean, I don't go *looking* for ghosts–I wouldn't recommend it; people tend to find things they go looking for–but now and again…

All three of these encounters happened in western settings, interestingly enough. I say "encounters" because I luckily don 't *see* ghosts; I know people who do and they mostly don't like it. I just… know they 're there, just as I'd know someone was in the room with me, even if I had my eyes closed.

Speaking of eyes closed…

One gentleman–I knew he was male–tried to get in bed with me at a conference hotel in Snowbird, Utah, of all unlikely places to be haunted. I was lying on my side, settling slowly toward sleep, when I felt the mattress give behind me, and someone lay down and put his arm around me. My initial drowsy thought was that it was my husband… and then I realized he wasn't with me; I was alone. Or supposed to be alone.

I flipped onto my back, blinking at the dark, and turned on the light. Nothing. Orderly, clean, impersonal hotel room. OK, I often see random things in my mind 's eye when drifting off to sleep… turned off the light, settled down again. And it happened again. Only I wasn't anywhere *near* asleep that time.

"Hey!" I said. "You stop that! I'm married!" Got up, turned on the light, fetched my rosary from my bag and put it down on the empty (well, "empty") side of the bed, then cautiously lay down again, one eye open, as it were. He seemed to have got the message, though, and didn't come back.

Another ghost was more recent, a couple of years ago. It wasn't a conscious encounter–I knew she was there, but she didn't sense me–but was disturbing. I 'd stopped at a roadside rest stop, on my way from Phoenix to Flagstaff, in the evening, and when I walked in, the women 's restroom was empty (unusual; it's a busy rest-stop). I pushed open the door of a cubicle, and walked straight into this woman. I couldn't see her, but dang, she was there.

She was relatively young and she was a mess, flailing and throwing herself at the walls. My best guess is that she 'd died in there of something like a drug overdose; she was bleary and incoherent, and definitely didn't know I was there. I backed straight out, of course, stood there (as one does) blinking for a few moments, then cautiously stuck my head back into the cubicle. Still there, an atmosphere of frenzy and despair. Really squalid way to go, poor thing.

I don 't set up to be an exorcist–like I say, I don 't go looking for these things–but the *only* thing I could do in the circumstances was to take a deep breath, step back inside and say a prayer for the peace of her soul. I mean, how can you leave somebody trapped in a public toilet without at least trying? So I did, and then stepped out, chose a different cubicle, and then left. I don 't know if she's still there or not; I haven 't gone back to look. I don 't want to meet her again, if she is.

The first ghost I met, though, was something quite different. It happened–reasonably enough–in the Alamo, in San Antonio. This was in 1990 or 91, just before *OUTLANDER* was released. I was attending a conference of the Romance Writers of America (or possibly the *Romantic Times* Convention, I forget) at the Menger Hotel, which is an old place, right across the street from the Alamo, which now stands in a small botanical park.

A friend had driven up from Houston to see me, and he suggested that we go walk through the Alamo, he being a botanist and therefore interested in the plants outside. He also thought I might find the building interesting. He said he 'd been there several times as a child, and had found it "evocative." So we strolled through the garden, looking at ornamental cabbages, and then went inside.

The present memorial is the single main church building, which is essentially no more than a gutted masonry shell. There's nothing at all in the church proper—a stone floor and stone walls, bearing the marks of hundreds of thousands of bullets; the stone looks chewed. There are a couple of smaller semi-open rooms at the front of the church, where the baptismal font and a small chapel used to be; these are separated from the main room by stone pillars and partial walls.

Around the edges of the main room are a few museum display cases, holding such artifacts of the defenders as the Daughters of Texas have managed to scrape together—rather a pitiful collection, including spoons, buttons, and (scraping the bottom of the barrel, if you ask me) a diploma certifying that one of the defenders had graduated from law school (this, like a number of other artifacts there, wasn't present in the Alamo during the battle, but was obtained later from the family of the man to whom it belonged).

The walls are lined with execrable oil paintings, showing the various defenders in assorted "heroic" poses. I suspect them all of having been executed by the Daughters of Texas in a special arts-and-crafts class held for the purpose, though I admit that I might be maligning the D of T by this supposition. At any rate, as museums go, this one doesn't.

It is quiet—owing to the presence of a young woman waving a "Silence, Please! THIS IS A SHRINE!" sign in the middle of the room—but is not otherwise either spooky or reverent in atmosphere. It's just a big, empty room. My friend and I cruised slowly around the room, making *sotto voce* remarks about the paintings and looking at the artifacts.

And then I walked into a ghost. He was near the front of the main room, about ten feet in from the wall, near the smaller room on the left (as you enter the church). I was surprised by this encounter, since a) I'd never met a ghost before; b) I hadn't expected to meet a ghost right then, and c) if I had, he wasn't what I would have expected.

I saw nothing, experienced no chill or feeling of oppression or malaise. The air felt slightly warmer where I stood, but not so much as to be really noticeable. The only really distinct feeling was one of... communication. Very distinct communication. I *knew* he was there—and he certainly knew *I* was. It was the feeling you get when you meet the eyes of a stranger and know at once this is someone you'd like.

I wasn't frightened in the least; just intensely surprised. I had a strong urge to continue standing there, "talking" (as it were; there were no words exchanged then) to this—man. Because it *was* a man; I could "feel" him distinctly and had a strong sense of his personality. I rather naturally assumed that I was imagining this, and turned to find my friend, to re-establish a sense of reality. He was about six feet away, and I started to walk toward him. Within a couple of feet, I lost contact with the ghost; couldn't feel him anymore. It was like leaving someone at a bus stop; a sense of broken communication.

Without speaking to my friend, I turned and went back to the spot where I had encountered the ghost. There he was. Again, he was quite conscious of me, too, though he didn't say anything in words. It was a feeling of "Oh, there you are!" on both parts.

I tried the experiment two or three more times–stepping away and coming back–with similar results each time. If I moved away, I couldn't feel him; if I moved back, I could. By this time, my friend was becoming understandably curious. He came over and whispered, "Is this what a writer does?", meaning to be funny. Since he evidently didn't sense the ghost–he was standing approximately where I had been–I didn't say anything about it, but merely smiled and went on outside with him, where we continued our botanical investigations.

The whole occurrence struck me as so very odd–while at the same time feeling utterly "normal"–that I went back to the Alamo–alone, this time–on each of the next two days. Same thing; he was there, in the same spot, and he knew me. Each time, I would just stand there, engaged in what I can only call mental communication. As soon as I left the spot–it was an area maybe two to three feet square–I couldn't sense him anymore.

I did wonder who he was, of course. There are brass plates at intervals around the walls of the church, listing the vital statistics of all the Alamo defenders, and I'd strolled along looking at these, trying to see if any of them rang a psychic bell, so to speak. None did.

Now, I did mention the occurrence to a few of the writers at the conference, all of whom were very interested. I don't think any of them went to the Alamo themselves–if they did, they didn't tell me–but more than one of them suggested that perhaps the ghost wanted me to tell his story, I being a writer and all. I said dubiously that I didn't *think* that's what he wanted, but the next–and last–time I went to the Alamo, I did ask him, in so many words.

I stood there and thought–consciously, in words–" What do you want? I can't really do anything for you. All I can give you is the knowledge that I know you're there; I care that you lived and I care that you died here."

And he *said*–not out loud, but I heard the words distinctly inside my head; it was the only time he spoke–he said, "That's enough."

At once, I had a feeling of completion. It *was* enough; that's all he wanted. I turned and went away. This time, I took a slightly different path out of the church, because there was a group of tourists in my way. Instead of leaving in a straight line to the door, I passed around the pillar dividing the main church from one of the smaller rooms. There was a small brass plate in the angle of the wall there, not visible from the main room.

The plate said that the smaller room had been used as a powder magazine during the defense of the fort. During the last hours of the siege, when it became apparent that the fort would fall, one of the defenders had made an effort to blow up the magazine, in order to destroy the fort and take as many of the attackers as possible with it. However, the man had been shot and killed just outside the smaller room, before he could succeed in his mission–more or less on the spot where I met the ghost.

So, I don 't know for sure; he didn't tell me his name, and I got no clear idea of his appearance–just a general impression that he was fairly tall; he spoke "down" to me, somehow. But for what it's worth, the man who was killed trying to blow up the powder magazine was named Robert Evans; he was described as being "black-haired, blue-eyed, nearly six feet tall, and always merry." That last bit sounds like the man I met, all right, but there's no telling.

Oddly enough, I did write about this man, indirectly. In *DRUMS OF AUTUMN*, a woman who's had an accident and found herself stranded in the wilderness overnight meets the ghost of an Indian, and… well, if Robert Evans is indeed the gentleman I met, I imagine he might find it entertaining.

I can't say how many–if any–of the unearthly encounters in this diverse collection might be based on some experience of the authors, or whether they derive purely from the realms of imagination. But I *can* say they're entertaining. Hope you enjoy them all!

–Diana Gabaldon

1

GHOSTED

Erin McCarthy

Rosie Lauer was a ghost hunter who had just been ghosted by a guy. The irony wasn't lost on her.

"Why do men do that?" she asked Santana, her co-host for their online show, *Got Ghosts*? "Seriously. I mean, if a guy doesn't want to date me anymore, can't he just say that? Instead of disappearing off the face of the earth?"

"Do you want a legitimate answer or a pat answer?" Santana asked, pushing her nerd glasses up on the bridge of her nose. The co-host for their show was one of the most intelligent human beings Rosie had ever met, and was a huge advocate for gender non-conformity and social equality.

Rosie stared out of the van window at the desert and shrugged, realizing she had chosen the wrong person to vent to about men being stereotypical commitment-phobes. Santana would want to have an actual dialogue about the complex subject when Rosie really just wanted someone to reassure her it was a genetic defect in men and she wasn't an undesirable ogre. "Pat answer, please."

Santana snorted as she drove. "Then the answer is this—men are afraid to tell the truth. And let's face it—a lot of women don't want to hear the truth."

"Fair enough." Rosie bit her fingernail, painted a bright blue. Maybe she didn't want the truth, because hello, the truth would hurt. She had *liked* Blaze Thibodeaux. In a very squishy-insides, giggly, panties-melting kind of way. His mother had been prescient in naming him Blaze because one crooked and charming smile from him and Rosie was on fire.

Sam, the cameraman who had replaced Blaze—because yes, Blaze had been apparently so repulsed by their date, he had quit his freaking *job*—leaned forward so he was in between their two seats. A big man with an even bigger beard, he was nice and efficient and kind of funny, but Rosie did not want to date him, or any other cameraman she had ever worked with besides Blaze. Nor did she want to get naked and rub bodies with Sam, even though she enjoyed his company, which was a great thing. Don't date co-workers, but have a quality working relationship with them. Sounds legit. Except she was pining for Blaze. Freaking *pining*.

"What the hell is that?" Sam asked, pointing through the windshield.

The landscape was a typical desert vista, brown and desolate. They were on the cusp of Death Valley, driving in to the ghost town of Rhyolite to film an episode for the show. Out of the shimmering heat, the mountains as a background, white undulating statues rose in front of them.

Rosie had done research on the site, so she knew the answer. "They're ghost statues by an artist depicting the Last Supper." They were way more eerie in person than in the pictures she had seen online though. There was a hint of something she would call "death shroud" to the design, and the white against the earth tones of the desert emulated sheet ghosts. In front of the few remaining dilapidated buildings of the former gold mining town, the statues were stark and mysterious. Altogether it was a lonely-ass location.

"Whose idea was that?" Sam asked, sounding amused. "Hey, let's throw up some creepy-as-fuck blobs in the desert?"

"It's art," Santana said. "I think they're very beautiful and expressive." She pulled the van up to the fence by the former general store. "Why is there another car here? No one else is supposed to meet us."

Rosie's heart started to race unnaturally fast. She was pretty damn sure she knew whose car that was. Not everyone had a bumper sticker that said, "I knit so I don't kill people." Blaze did, because he had bought the car from an eccentric eighty-year-old woman in Reno and had refused to remove it, finding it hilarious.

Which meant he hadn't quit his job.

She wasn't sure how to feel about that.

Opening the passenger door to the van, she did the leap down that short girls have to make. The world in general seemed designed for those vertically gifted. Like Blaze. He was tall. And dark. And really damn handsome.

As the heat hit her with all the subtlety of a dog jumping up on her leg, Rosie picked at the front of her T-shirt and hauled her bag out of the front seat, trying not to wince at the last text she had sent Blaze.

Can't wait to see you again.

It had felt natural. After three months of working together, a friendship and attraction blooming slowly and naturally, he had asked her out. They had gone to the beach, which had been risky because a bathing suit on a first date made a woman vulnerable. But it had been a great day and they had laughed, and he had kissed her passionately at her door, and she had pictured a blissful future where they offended friends with their sheer adorableness as a couple and people jokingly referred to them as "Bosie" or "Raze" because they were always together.

Yeah. She had gone there. From zero to ninety, which was not something she normally did.

Then he hadn't answered that text. Or shown up for work. For three days.

Which upon reflection wasn't really that long, but in terms of modern technology it was an infinity.

Now he was here and she was mortified. Torn between the urge to kick him in the dick and throw herself at him and stick to his chest like a starfish. The first she might do. The second she swore she wouldn't. Though maybe she should instruct Santana to murder her if she did.

She didn't usually embarrass herself with men. Seriously. But this guy...

He came out of the furthest building suddenly, filling the doorway with his broad shoulders and impressive biceps. Lord, the man could fill a pair of jeans to perfection.

So she did the only thing she could under the circumstances.

She pretended to not see him and ran into the nearest building, palms sweating and mouth hot.

3

So much for dignity.

"What is wrong with you?" Rosie whispered to herself as she dropped her bag on the dusty wood floor of a crumbling building. "You just ran away from Blaze, oh my God. You ran away, you complete and total loser."

But she had needed a minute to regroup. Be nonchalant. Cool as a freaking cucumber, that was her. In a second. After her heart slid back down her throat into her chest where it belonged.

"Clara?" a male voice called from another room. "Clara?"

Rosie jumped. Great, someone had heard her muttering to herself. "Um, no, it's Rosie Lauer from *Got Ghosts?* Are you the property manager?" She wiped her sweaty palms down the front of her jeans and vowed to stop being an idiot.

She was a professional ghost hunter, damn it, and people took her seriously.

Sort of, anyway. She had established her career on the shtick of being afraid of literally everything. Santana was afraid of nothing. Rosie shrieked like a banshee on the regular. Viewers loved it.

She had yet to really be truly terrified of anything.

Until she shoved open a door, passed through the doorway and saw a ghost.

* * *

He tried to go to her, to reach her, protect her. Clara. She was screaming in the darkness. He could smell the acrid sting of gun powder, and feel the bloom of pain in his chest. He tried to run. "Clara?"

It was always like this. The gunshot, the screams, the pain, the smoke.

And he could never get to his beloved. His movements were weak, ineffectual, met with resistance, like trying to run in the mud at the bottom of the river. His feet were rooted, his hands never close enough to push the door open so he could get to her. Save her. See her.

Always out of reach, and out of sight. Time spun endlessly, days and years knitting together, until he felt weighted down by the fabric of eternity.

Then suddenly the door slammed open in front of him, and for the first time in his endless quest for contact with his love, he saw something. Something other than the wood floor, the dusty walls, and the rise of gunpowder smoke from a weapon he never saw, but seemed to fire endlessly in the mystery of his living dream-like existence.

The only thing that ever felt real was his pain.

Until now.

Until he saw a woman standing in front of him, dressed like a man.

* * *

Rosie let out a shriek. There was a man in front of her. Not a live man. Not a solid form. But a spirit. A ghost. A dead guy.

Here heart was in her throat and she stood there, frozen, like she'd stumbled upon a black bear three feet away. Taking a deep breath, she reminded herself that unlike a bear, a ghost couldn't hurt her. This man was dead.

He was hovering transparent, like a hologram.

Hell, maybe it wasn't a ghost. Maybe he was a projection, part of the site's attractions. Like a dead gold miner tour guide.

She inched into the room, darting her gaze around to see if she could spot a projector or a staff member. "Hello?" she asked, cautiously, her voice sounding insanely booming in the still room.

It was dusty, undisturbed. It looked like it had been at least several days since anyone had been in the building. Rosie stuck her hand out and tried to put it right through the hologram.

Only when she did the man's eyes widened in shock, and she felt like she'd just crammed her hand into a meat locker. It was ice cold.

Rosie jerked back, and the man disappeared. He faded, like cigarette smoke in the wind. That was weird. Heart pounding, she assessed the room again, wishing she had her equipment on her. Over the years doing the show she had seen mild evidence that spirits could exist, but nothing irrefutable. As she wandered around the room now, she was officially freaked out.

Shit had just gotten real.

She decided to go back to the van and grab her iPad and actually read the background on this place and who was supposed to be the resident spirit. She had neglected her research because she'd been preoccupied with Blaze and his electric kiss.

Speak of the devil. As she walked through the door, he was walking in, and she collided with him. "Blaze, oh my God, sorry! What are you doing here?"

Don't babble, she mentally coached herself. Be strong. Be confident.

He gave her a smile that would convince a nun to sin. "Hey, Rosie. What do you mean, what am I doing here? This is my job."

He touched both of her arms, holding her steady so she wouldn't stumble. And left his hands there, where his warm touch caused goose bumps to spring up on her bare arms. He was distracting her with both his sexiness and his words. "But Santana said that Julie said no one had heard from you in three days. That you no-showed for reshoots day before yesterday."

And then he ghosted her.

His eyebrows shot up. Blaze had green eyes and dark, short hair. A trim, masculine beard. "What are you talking about? I came out here with Julie. She's the one who told me I wasn't needed for reshoots. That was... Monday."

The day after their date. "What? That doesn't make any sense." Julie was the show's producer. She was the kind of woman who refused to acknowledge she was aging, insisted constantly men were hitting on her and harassing her, when usually they'd offered a mere greeting, and was ridiculously dramatic about minor ailments she contracted. Maybe she had gotten her wires crossed somehow, but that wasn't like her. Usually she was a brutal control freak. But whatever.

Rosie tried to take a step back, unnerved by his closeness and his smile.

"I need you to grab your camera," she said. "I think there is some activity in this room. Do you have any idea what this building was?"

For a second she didn't think he was going to either release her or answer her. That he was just going to stand there and hypnotize her with his hotness while she forgot anything else existed in the world except for him.

But then he just released her and said, "Be right back." He hesitated briefly before turning around and leaving. But almost immediately he stopped and turned back around. "Can I ask you a question?"

As long as it didn't involve her secret hopes and dreams and whether or not she was currently undressing him with her eyes, because she was. "Sure."

Then in the world's most infuriating behavior he shook his head with a scuff and a smile. "Never mind."

Blaze left and Rosie wanted to kick his perfect backside with her boot. What the hell? Could he torment her any more?

* * *

Joining the show three months ago had been a fun change of pace for Blaze after doing some heavy docudrama work in Vegas. He loved his job and the challenge of a new setting every few weeks and a new vibe. Plus it had the bonus of the adorable star of the show, Rosie, who he had been watching online for at least a year. There was something so damn cute about her. He had to admit she had influenced his decision to go for this job. As he went out to his truck he wondered why she seemed so nervous around him. Obviously she had an entirely different opinion of their lone date and the kiss he had given her at the end of the night on her doorstep.

For him? Boom. Fireworks.

But Rosie hadn't texted him and when she had laid eyes on him just now her expression looked like she'd been sucking on a fresh-cut lemon.

That was not the sucking he had envisioned between them.

It was rare for him to devote this much time and thought to asking a woman out, but they worked together and that had been concerning. But each week that went by, he had seen both their friendship and their chemistry grow until he was totally preoccupied with thoughts of Rosie twenty-four seven. His pre-employment interest had turned into a full-on desire and deep respect.

So, he'd asked her out. They'd had a great time, and now she was pretending the date had never occurred. Being blown off did not feel great, and he wasn't going to let her off the hook that easy. Never say Blaze Thibodeaux didn't go down fighting.

What he wanted to go down on was her.

Santana was unloading bags and studying the layout of the town. "Hey, what's up? I thought you were MIA."

"Why is everyone saying that? Julie told me not to show up. So I didn't." Blaze was bewildered by that. Julie was the one who had gotten him the job in the first place, having worked with him on a previous show.

"Oh, okay, cool. No big deal. I guess wires got crossed." Santana blew her bangs out of her eyes. "Did you see Rosie? Did she say where she wants to start? I think we should go in the remains of the train depot. Rumor has it a woman was murdered there. Her lover tried to save her but he was shot too."

"I saw Rosie in that building." He pointed. "She said there was activity."

Santana's eyebrows rose. "She did? That's weird. Rosie never thinks there is activity."

He grinned. "I know. For being jumpy as hell on camera she really is a huge skeptic."

"Let's go. This is going to be interesting."

* * *

Rosie just blinked as she stared down the barrel of a hunting rifle. She was so shocked that she couldn't even react, confusion almost outweighing her fear. "Is this a joke?" she asked. "Am I being punked?"

Because why else would the producer of their show be glaring at her, rifle raised, hand on the trigger?

"No, you are not. But don't worry," Julie said. "I'm not going to shoot you. This is just a friendly warning so you understand the seriousness of what I'm about to say."

Rosie couldn't believe her producer was insane. Sure, she had never been a huge fan of Julie's, because the woman tended to be a little too intense and random, but she hadn't thought she was certifiable. This was a whole new level of crazy. She swallowed hard and inched to the right slightly. Maybe she could dive through the open-air window and run like hell.

"Sure," she said, hoping she sounded soothing and complacent. "What can I do for you, Julie?"

"You can leave Blaze alone."

Um, what? Rosie froze in her miniscule sideways shuffle. "What are you talking about?"

"He's mine, Rosie. Mine. And I made sure to delete all your texts to him so that he would think you blew him off. But then I had to listen to him talking about you endlessly and insist on being here for this shoot so I figured this was my best option."

She had never thought of herself as slow on the uptake but what the actual hell? Blaze hadn't ghosted her? Julie was a crazy stalker? "Fine. Done. I'll leave him alone," she said, her heart racing. "Put that gun down, someone is going to come in here any second now."

At least she hoped they were. Where the hell were Blaze and Santana?

It was neither of them who actually appeared in the doorway. It was Sam. "Hey, Rosie, can I grab a—"

His sentence cut off and he screamed.

Julie whirled, astonished. "Who are you?"

Rosie secretly hoped Sam was really an undercover cop who would throw Julie on the ground and arrest her, but that didn't happen. For a split second she debated hurling herself at Julie's back and tackling her but she didn't know if the gun was loaded or not. It could accidentally go off and she couldn't risk that.

So she stayed frozen. Sam, clearly not a double agent, dropped to the ground with his hands over his head as he continued to scream, and Blaze came bursting through the door, Santana on his heels.

"It's a prop," Julie growled, pointing it at Sam. "Shut the hell up!"

"What is going on here?" Blaze demanded, reaching out and yanking the rifle out of Julie's hands in what Rosie thought was single-handedly the sexiest thing she had ever seen in her life.

He checked to see if it was loaded and did whatever it was you were supposed to do to secure it. Rosie had zero experience with weapons. But seeing him in control made her heart dislodge from her throat and return to her chest where it belonged. Geez, Louise, Julie was loony, and she was now fairly certain that had not been a prop, but the real thing.

Rosie was about to attempt an explanation, despite the fact that she wasn't exactly sure herself what the hell had just happened, when a cold wave of air rolled over her. She closed her eyes and shuddered, unnerved by the intense sensation of being dipped into a barrel of ice water.

A shudder rolled up her spine and her fingers trembled. She popped her eyes open. "Did anyone feel that?" she gasped.

But before anyone could give a response, Julie went sprawling forward, as if she had been pushed, her head cracking with the doorframe. She went down with no sound other than the rustle of her clothes.

"What is going on?" Sam cried out.

Blaze rushed to Julie. "She's unconscious. Did she trip?"

No. Rosie could see the ghostly figure from before hovering in the space behind Julie. He turned, gave her a sad smile and a wink, and disappeared.

* * *

"Next time I'm going to actually do my prep," Rosie said as she sat on the floor of the bank building and listened to Santana's story of William and Clara, the star-crossed lovers from the mining town's glory days.

"So basically, before there was such a word, William had a stalker. A crazy former prostitute turned saloon owner in the red light district. She killed William's girlfriend, Clara, right in front of him, then shot him."

Rosie shuddered and cast a sidelong glance at Blaze. They were on the side of the building that no longer had a wall, so their legs were dangling over the edge, her feet bumping against the foundation. "That's horrible." She put her hand on Blaze's leg. "Are you okay?"

He gave her a look of astonishment. "Me? I'm fine. I'm more worried about you. She could have killed you!" Blaze laced his fingers through hers. "I don't even know if I could live with myself if something had happened to you and it was my fault."

"It wasn't your fault!"

"Julie was clearly insane," Santana confirmed.

"I just meant it must be upsetting to realize you had a stalker," Rosie said. "That's creepy."

"What's creepier is I had no idea. I seriously had no idea she had watched me enter my password and gone and deleted my texts from you. That's just ... crazy train."

Santana jumped down onto the hard-packed dirt. The sun was starting to set. "I'm going to go check the audio. Be back in a few."

"I guess we have a show to film," Rosie said, nudging Blaze's knee. "You sure you don't mind working?" Sam had bailed, getting a lift back with the police who had arrested Julie.

"No. That's what I came here to do." He turned and gave her a smile. "And to see you."

"Really? And here I thought you ghosted me." The temperature was finally dropping and the sun was dropping behind the mountains. This would be a perfect time for Blaze to kiss her again.

"I would never ghost you. Trust me on this. I think you are the most adorable, hilarious, and sweetest woman I've met in a long time." His eyes were smoldering as he reached out and cupped her cheek with rough, masculine hands. "I'm going to kiss you."

"You better," she breathed. "I've been waiting forever for you to kiss me again."

The corner of his mouth turned up. "It's been four days."

Rosie nodded. "Exactly. Forever."

Then Blaze covered her mouth with his and she forgot everything about space and time.

* * *

Blaze kept Rosie firmly by his side, despite the way she was blushing a little as Santana assessed them curiously. He squeezed her hand. That kiss had been even better than the first.

Fireworks finale.

But Santana had called them to listen to the audio.

They were in the van, listening to it on the laptop away from the wind of the desert.

"Hear that?" Santana asked.

He nodded. "'Clara.' It's a man's voice saying 'Clara.'"

Rosie's eyes widened. "I heard it too. That's wild. So you think this was William calling out for his girlfriend?"

"Oh, wait, it gets better." Santana pushed her glasses up on the bridge of her nose and forwarded the recording ahead by seven minutes. "Here."

"William." This time a woman's voice, sounding relieved.

"She answered him," Blaze said, awed. "It's crystal clear."

"I hope they're together," Rosie said.

Blaze swallowed the sudden lump in his throat and gave in to the urge to kiss the top of Rosie's head. "Yeah. Me too."

The smoke cleared for the first time in a hundred years and there she was. Clara.

11

William had seen the gun. Seen the woman pointing it at the short woman with the curls.

The injustice, the rage, had filled him and he had moved forward with a burst of energy.

She had felled like a tree.

And there was Clara. Blond and beautiful and no longer bleeding.

He reached his hand for her. She smiled and took it.

They walked down the steps and into the thriving town and into eternity.

2

LOST AND FOUND

Leah Snow

The Territory of Utah: 1865

Katherine was jostled awake as the wagon creaked and bucked over the rough ground. Deciding she might as well get up, she crawled over the crates and luggage to the rear of the wagon and lowered herself over the back and down onto the trail. She smoothed her dress out as best she could, shook out her long dark hair, gathered it, and tied it up. She felt guilty about napping during the day, but she'd barely slept last night.

It was late afternoon, the western sun just touching the distant mountain tops, the sky all soft purples and red and oranges. She stared at the mountains, so far away. *That's where we're heading,* Katherine thought. *That's where I can start over.* A fresh start. A new life. That's exactly what she needed. And that was why she had hitched a ride on the wagon train heading to Sacramento.

From there she could travel to San Francisco fairly easily. The whole trip was somewhat daunting, truth be told, as Katherine had never left Utah before. Had never been out of Ogden, in fact. This was all so new, so frightening, but at the same time, freeing.

* * *

The daughter of a farmer, Katherine's early life had been difficult, but school had saved her. Miss Benedict, the schoolmistress, had seen something in Katherine; a desire to *know*, to seek information about life outside of her tight-knit community. Katherine stayed after school with Miss Benedict many times, straightening the tables, wiping the slates, but more importantly, reading, learning math, and had even borrowed chapbooks on occasion. Until her brother Toby found them and showed to them to Father.

"There's no reason for you be learning to read and write!" he had thundered. "You think you're too good for us?"

"No, Father," she replied, head down. But the truth was, she *did* think she was better than them. Toby and her other three brothers were content working the farm, while Katherine was obligated to spend day after day washing, cleaning, cooking, feeding the livestock, and of course, at prayer.

Her mother was sullen and quiet. If she ever had a personality, it had been washed out of her long ago. She gave Katherine no guidance or advice, other than how her father preferred his breakfast.

Katherine took solace in the books, far-off adventures and mysterious places. Until the books had been taken away and thrown into the fire. She had been forbidden to go back to school.

After that, there was the farm and the endless work. Day after day. Her only social life was church, but even then, there was little freedom, only brief moments for bursts of girlish laughter and whispered, excited gossip with her few friends.

Then she met Thomas Parker. He was wealthy, charming, and handsome. Tall with dark blond hair and beautiful blue eyes. The other girls blushed when Thomas strode down the aisle at church and nodded at them. They set their sights on him. But Thomas had selected her. Her.

The Parkers owned several buildings in town, and Thomas worked at the bank until fall, when he planned to study law back East.

That is, until he met Katherine. His plans changed. Their plans changed. They would live in a little house just outside of town, he told her. He would open a dry goods store. She would work there too. She was so good with numbers. So smart. So beautiful.

He spoke sweetly, his perfect lips so close, breathing his vows and promises in her ear.

And when she told him she was with child, Thomas had taken it so well. She was so relieved. He held her hands, looked into her eyes, and promised to speak to his father, and then the justice of the peace. And she had believed him. Everything.

"My darling," he said, his eyes holding hers, "we'll be married within the week." And he had left her on her porch, her heart bursting with love and her eyes brimming with tears of happiness.

She never saw Thomas again. He left on an early train that next morning, presumably headed East. Her father had dressed in his Sunday best and took the wagon to the Parker home in order to speak with Thomas's father, but had not even made it to the front porch. Several armed men, employees of the Parkers, escorted him from the property.

Katherine's family never spoke of it.

Her father, if he happened to look in her direction, would glare. He only spoke to her to issue commands. Her brothers followed their father's lead and avoided her altogether. Her mother pulled even farther away.

Her pregnancy was long and lonely. Only the baby growing inside her belly to keep her company.

One night at supper, she looked around the table from face to face: her father wearing his permanent scowl, her brothers shoveling food into their mouths as fast as they could. Her mother, pinched and worn, quiet as a shadow. None of them speaking. No warmth. No love. She put her hand on her round stomach, which elicited a scowl from her younger brother.

I can't bring a daughter into this, Katherine thought.

She left late that night. No note. No goodbyes. She hitched a ride to Salt lake City, paying with twenty dollars stolen from the metal box kept in the kitchen cabinet. A wagon train was leaving in two days and she joined it.

The baby was born late one night, only three weeks into the journey; early by all accounts. Two of the older women tended to her. They lay Katherine on the ground, atop several blankets, away from the rest of the settlers.

It was painful, so painful. Katherine screamed, reached for a hand to hold, for something, but the women were occupied, whispering to each other, urgency in their tones. Eventually, Katherine blacked out.

The baby was born dead. One of the women laid the child in Katherine's arms and stood over her. "You say your goodbyes now.

15

I'll be back for her in a minute."

Her? A daughter. Katherine held her daughter and looked her over, the perfect, sweet face, her tiny hands, curled into powerless fists.

She felt numb. She had never experienced sorrow as deep as this. She was empty inside, body and soul, and so, so tired. She closed her eyes and fell into deep, welcome darkness.

After several minutes, the woman returned, knelt beside her, and removed the child from her arms and walked toward the sound of a shovel cutting dirt.

Katherine awoke, cold and alone in the darkness. She called out for someone, her mother, but there was no response. She heard muted voices from the campfire. She drifted off again.

* * *

"Hold up!" Sully, the guide, shouted, riding back along the wagons. "We'll set up here for the night." The wagons slowed, and Katherine looked around. The area was flat, except for a few rocky outcroppings and low, spindly bushes. It was easy to see for miles in every direction. A narrow creek ran nearby, sheltered by a handful of struggling trees.

Sully rode to the first wagon, spoke to the driver, who tugged on the reins, pulling the oxen into a sharp right turn. Slowly, awkwardly, the other wagons followed his lead, and soon, with minimal shouting from Sully (they were getting better at it every day, thought Katherine), they formed a rough circle.

The oxen lowed and kicked the dirt and hung their big heads.

The children climbed down from the wagons and a boy and a girl ran around with a small dog, laughing and shouting.

The women began passing down pots and pans, supplies for supper.

The menfolk untied the oxen and horses and led them to the stream.

Tanner, the driver/cook/blacksmith set to stacking wood and building a fire. Sully rode around some more, scouting the area. He rode to the stream, let his horse splash around, much to the delight of the children, and then tied it to a low hanging branch and came back to the camp.

* * *

Supper was done (beans and biscuits again) and the daily chores completed, and most of the adults sat around the fire, talking softly. Katherine sat close to the fire, warming her hands. It seemed to her as though the nights were getting colder. One of the menfolk stood up and pointed. "Look there!"

The others turned, some standing to see better. A line of riders, their shapes dark and hard to make out against the blackening sky, approached the camp. There were at least a dozen of them.

"Who are they?" one of the women said, fear evident in her voice.

Sully stood, staring at the approaching figures. He turned to one of the men. "Joseph, you and Daniel gather up the horses and tie them to the wagons. And somebody get the kids out of sight."

Several settlers ran off to comply, their footsteps loud in the sudden silence.

"Who are they?" the woman asked again.

Tanner moved beside Sully, whispered something to him. Sully nodded. Tanner, walked toward the riders.

They were Indians. Strong, proud, dangerous, their dark skin and painted faces even more menacing in the flickering firelight. They looked at the wagons and over at the pioneers with disdain.

"Paiutes," Sully said.

Tanner approached them, hands raised to his shoulders, and spoke quietly. The Paiute warriors kicked and guided their horses until they surrounded him. One of the Indians gave a terrifying war cry, and gestured at the wagons. Another, an older man, his long gray hair braided, spoke and the brave quieted.

A woman beside Katherine said, "What do they want?"

"I'm not sure," Katherine said.

"Sully, should we get the guns?" a short, red-faced man asked.

"Just keep still," Sully said. "Nobody do anything stupid."

In one smooth, practiced movement, an Indian leapt off his horse, spun Tanner around and struck him with a club. Tanner went to his knees, the Indian hit him again, and Tanner fell onto his face. The Indian turned and faced the small group gathered at the fire and let out another cry.

One of the women screamed, and Sully muttered, "Oh boy."

"What are we supposed to do now?" the red-faced farmer said.

17

"We don't do nothing, "Sully said. "There's too many of 'em. And the way they see it, this is their land. Their rules."

"What are they going to do?" a man said, pulling his wife close.

Several more Indians had jumped down from their horses and approached the wagons. One leapt into the back of the wagon and they heard him rummaging around, occasionally a box or item of clothing flew out the back of the wagon. They heard glass break. A woman put her hands up to her mouth and murmured a prayer through her clasped hands.

The leader sat on his horse, impassive, not joining in, but not stopping them.

Two of the braves approached the group huddled around the campfire. One of them grabbed a handful of a woman's long blond hair and ran it through his fingers. The woman squeezed her eyes tight, fought back tears. Sully put a restraining hand on her husband's arm.

The Indian turned and barked something to his companion, who laughed. Then his eyes met Katherine's. His laughter stopped. He released the woman's hair. Katherine shrank away as he approached her.

A scream shattered the air, and the brave turned. Katherine ran from the fire and ducked into the darkness between two wagons.

One of the older girls, Destiny, Katherine thought her name was, was pulled from a wagon. Her father leapt up to protest, and an Indian held up his rifle. The father stopped.

"We have to do something, "one of the men hissed.

"Is that another one?" someone said.

A single rider was approaching, but from the west. Katherine stepped forward for a better look. He didn't look like an Indian. The shape of his Stetson and his long duster indicated that much.

He passed between the wagons close to where Katherine was hiding, slowed his horse and looked down at her. She couldn't make out his face, just the shape. Broad shoulders, dark hair that fell past his collar. And dark green eyes that caught the firelight.

"Best stay there, miss," he said, his voice low and rough.

The stranger moved closer to the fire and got off his horse. He handed the reins to Sully. The Indian holding the men at rifle point swiveled his gun up, but the stranger paid him no mind. He strode purposefully across the camp, his hands held away from his guns as the Indians moved in around him.

The stranger approached the fallen form of Tanner and knelt beside him, spoke briefly. Tanner moved ever so slightly.

The stranger stood and spoke sharply to the leader.

Katherine couldn't make out what he was saying, but she could hear enough to know they weren't speaking English. The big brave, the one who had struck Tanner, moved quickly, chest to chest with the stranger. He looked at the leader and gesticulated and shouted. The stranger stood there, tall and stoic. His eyes never left the leader's face.

The leader issued a harsh command. He looked at his men and spoke sharply, gestured at the group huddled by the fire.

The other braves dropped their loot and climbed back on the horses. The cowboy spoke briefly to the chief, who nodded, turned, and kicked his horse forward. The others turned and followed.

They were soon lost in the night, and after several moments, even their hoofbeats faded away.

The stranger helped Tanner to his feet, and with an arm around his waist, led him to the fireside.

Sully and one of the farmers helped him to a stool. Sully looked at the ugly bruise on his forehead and mopped up a trickle of blood that ran down the side of his face.

"He got you pretty good, huh?" he said.

Tanner smiled ruefully. "That's the hardest I've been hit in a long time." He looked up at the stranger. "Thanks, mister. What'd you say to them?"

His voice was low, and Katherine had to move closer to hear him.

"I told them you were just passing through. That you meant no harm, and that they should leave you be."

"Just like that?" asked Sully.

"Just like that." the stranger said. He got to his feet and tipped his hat. "I'll be heading off now. They won't trouble you no more. But I wouldn't linger once it gets light, if you catch my meaning."

"Wait," Sully said. "Stay and have a cup of coffee." He winked. "Or a snort of whiskey, if you'd rather?"

The tall stranger's mouth twisted in a ghost of a smile. "That's mighty tempting, but I've got to head out. I'll be keeping an eye out for you folks."

His eyes moved toward Katherine, then back to the group at the fire.

Katherine stepped forward, hand outstretched, fingers grasping. She stopped. What was she doing? What was she going to say?

She watched his dim figure fade into the darkness, then stared for a long time into the night.

"Who was that?" asked one of the farmers. His voice was quiet, as if he was afraid the stranger would hear him.

Sully tamped tobacco in his pipe. "That depends on who you ask. I've heard his name is Walker. He has a cabin somewhere round these parts."

"He lives *out here?*" a woman said. "In the middle of nowhere?"

Tanner took a swallow from a flask, offered it to one of the farmers, who refused with a shake of his head.

Sully lit his pipe, puffed, threw the match in the fire. "His two boys, I believe it was, were killed by Paiutes a few years back. The three of them were headed West, just like you folks, and were set upon. Stories say he stays here to be with them."

"Be with them?" the woman asked.

"Their spirits," Sully said.

"People say he can talk to ghosts," Tanner added, poking the embers with a stick. He gazed into the fire, the flames reflected in his eyes. He looked up. "That his sons visit him sometimes. That's why he doesn't leave. There's even some that say that *he's* a ghost."

Sully nodded. "Yup. I heard that too."

"A ghost?" Katherine said. He didn't look like a ghost. Not that she would know.

"Ghosts," said a farmer. "That's nonsense. Ain't no such thing."

Some of the others nodded in agreement.

"Pardon me for saying," Sully said, "But I couldn't help noticing that most of you folks carry around Bibles and all."

"What of it?" demanded a farmer.

"Well," Sully took a drag on his pipe. "I ain't no scholar or nothing, but aren't there mention of ghosts in the Bible? A Holy Ghost?"

"Well that's not the same thing."

"Isn't it?" Sully said.

Beneath his broad-brimmed hat, still looking down at the fire, Tanner smiled. Katherine caught it, and she smiled too. She was so tired of self-righteous people, always telling you how you should live your life. Like her father and her brothers. And most times, their own lives were full of lies and misery. Her father rarely smiled.

But why think about them? That was her old life. That life was over.

She yawned and turned from the fire and went to find a place to lie down. Maybe she would be able to sleep tonight.

* * *

She saw him again two days later. It was early morning and she was one of the first ones up. She made her way through the waking camp. Hushed voices from a wagon as she passed. A woman at the fire preparing breakfast. Two of the men were tending to the oxen, but they paid her no mind as she walked by them. She strolled away from the campsite toward the sun, rising low and orange in the east.

A figure stood on a low hill, beside a horse. She started for a moment, thinking it was an Indian, but then she saw his long coat flapping. It was *him*. She knew it. Was he looking at her? Or at the camp itself? She raised a tentative hand and waved, then pulled it back in, self-conscious and shy. If he saw, he made no sign. The sun rose fully behind him, the brightness causing her to squint and turn away.

When she looked back, he was gone. He had disappeared. Like a ghost.

* * *

The chores were done, and there was a brief respite before supper. Quiet laughter from the women by the cooking pot. A guitar played (badly) beneath the squeals of children at play. Katherine stood in the shallow stream, her bare feet in the water. It was cold, but the water and the soft mud beneath it felt good, soothing, after another long day of walking along the wagons.

The days seemed to blend together; yesterday, the day before that, and the ones prior to that, drifting back to the day they left Salt Lake City. Walking, occasionally riding, sleeping, more walking. It was hard to remember how long they had been traveling. The days and nights blurred together.

They still had a few more weeks to go, Tanner had said that at

21

breakfast, before looking up at the threatening sky and announcing they were heading into a storm.

It had been overcast all day, but the rain hadn't started yet. For the moment, the sun was shining through a hole in the cloud cover, and she let it wash over her. She had been so cold lately, and the warmth of the sun felt so good. She closed her eyes and let her head fall back, relaxing, soaking in the sunlight, thinking of nothing.

"Be careful you don't fall in," a voice said.

She jerked her head up, blinked her eyes open, stumbled over a smooth, slippery rock, lost her balance and would have fallen in, but a strong, rough hand grasped her forearm and steadied her.

It was him. Walker. She regained her footing and he let go of her arm. She was conscious of how warm and safe his hand had felt on her arm. She could still feel the touch of his fingers.

He was shirtless, his muscular, tan chest glistening with water.

"Sorry about that," he said with a slight smile. "I didn't mean to startle you."

"Oh, no," she said. "It's, I'm… it's fine." She looked at his face, but her eyes were drawn back to his bare torso, lean and muscular. A cruel white scar stood out across his stomach, and she wondered how he had gotten it. Her fingers wanted to touch it, the pale curved line that crossed his belly just above his navel. She looked down at her feet.

She scolded herself. *Why are you acting like this?*

"What are you doing here?" she asked. Not accusing, just curious.

"I told you I'd be keeping an eye on you," he said, turning and pulling his shirt on over his head. She risked another look. His back too, was hard and lean.

"Our guide said you live out here. Is that true?"

He smoothed back his wet hair and nodded. He knelt and opened a canteen and filled it up. He sat back on his haunches and looked at her.

"So, you're heading to California?"

She nodded, shy now that his focus was on her.

"Why?"

The question was so bare, so utterly naked that she wasn't sure how to answer.

"Where are your people?" he said. He nodded toward the

wagons. "Are you traveling with them?"

She shook her head, not meeting his gaze.

He stood up and slapped his hat on his thigh, sending dust into the air. "Didn't mean to upset you. My apologies."

She stepped toward him. "Wait. No. I'm sorry."

She moved in front of him. His dark green eyes, long lashes, beneath thick black hair that needed a combing. He had several days growth of beard. He was a handsome man, to be sure. But there was more. Something in his eyes. Something sad. His sons? Was that story true?

His eyebrows rose with the unanswered question.

"I'm not sure how to respond," she said. "It's complicated. Part of why I'm going to California is to get away, and part of it is to start over. I'm not sure which it is."

"Why not both?" he said, smiling gently. "Sometimes you need to get away to start over. Otherwise you just keep on repeating the same mistakes." His eyes stayed on hers, and she remembered how his hand had felt on her arm. She wanted to feel that again.

"Don't you get lonely out here? All by yourself?" She asked it before she thought about it. Women weren't supposed to ask such questions. Would he think she was being rude? Too forward?

He met her eyes and rubbed his chin. "Sometimes," he said. "Sometimes I get lonely. But I have—"

A drop of water hit her cheek. They both glanced up. The sky had definitely darkened, the heavy clouds dark and threatening, now overhead. The patter of raindrops hitting the ground and leaves began, picked up intensity. Sully's storm.

He put his hat on and picked up the reins. "I'd get under cover if I were you. This might be a bad one." He pulled himself aboard his horse in a strong, practiced motion. He tugged the reins and the horse turned. He looked down at her and touched his hat. "Ma'am. Until next time."

She nodded, gave a tentative smile, not noticing the rain driving harder, pelting her, until he was out of sight. She picked up her boots and ran barefoot back to camp.

That night, lying on a bedroll in the cramped provision wagon, as the wind and rain battered the canvas cover, she wondered what he was going to say. "But I have–" What? A wife?

* * *

23

The rain continued throughout the next day, steady and unrelenting. And the next. For nearly a week it rained.

The trail became mud, the wagon wheels churning, sometimes not finding purchase, the oxen leaning and struggling, moving seemingly an inch at a time. The stream they followed grew every day, and Katherine caught snatches of enough conversations to know that crossing the river was going to be harder than they had planned.

Everything was wet. Most of the settlers didn't bother changing clothes because everything was soaked. And if you did put on something dry, it would be drenched within minutes. Dinners were cold biscuits and cold coffee. Several of the children coughed and sniffled and cried all night. Everyone was in a foul mood, and only spoke if necessary. It reminded her of life at home, and she stayed by herself more than usual.

Each time the rain let up, she looked around for Walker. He said he'd be watching out for them. Was he still? She hoped so.

Katherine went barefoot most of the time. It was easier. The mud did everything it could to suck the boots right off her feet.

On the fifth (or was it the sixth?) day, the rain stopped. It eased to a steady drizzle, and then it just stopped. Their spirits lifted, even though the going was still slow and arduous, but that night, for the first time in seemingly forever, they had a hot meal.

After dinner, sitting near the others at the fire, their voices eager as they spoke of their plans for California, Katherine gazed away from the fire, away from the others, into the darkness. Was she still looking for Walker? She wondered if they would ever meet again.

* * *

Katherine couldn't sleep. She flopped to her side, gazing up at the underside of the supply wagon. It had not rained for several days, and the ground had dried out. She preferred sleeping outside. The wagons were too closed.

She closed her eyes and tried again.

Soft voices came from one of the other wagons. A coyote howled from somewhere in the distance. A lonely cry. A sad cry.

Enough. Katherine sat up. Something was bothering her. What it was, she couldn't say. But something was out there... calling... waiting for her.

She slid from beneath the wagon. She looked around. Two

figures standing by the fire, but they were looking the other way.

Staying tight against the wagon, close in the shadow, she made her way to the outside of the circle of wagons. She was restless and felt like walking. Where? She wasn't sure. But somewhere. The moon was clear and bright, a hazy ring around it.

Katherine half-walked, half-crawled up a steep rise, using her hands and feet. Rocks and pebbles fell, rattling beneath her and she worried that the men by the fire would hear.

Then she was atop a hill overlooking the wagons. She got to her feet and dusted off her dress and looked around.

The camp lay just below her. Stars above. So many of them. She'd always been interested in the stars and planets, but her father wouldn't hear of it. Nonsense. A waste of time.

She gazed off in the distance, into the darkness, away from the firelight. What was that? A light? Another fire? Her first thought was the Indians. Or another group of settlers.

But something told her it was him. *Walker*. Hadn't Sully said he lived out here?

Without thinking about it, she began walking toward the light.

It was easy to see in the moonlight, and she moved quickly. Another coyote cried out. It suddenly occurred to her how foolish and downright dangerous this was. But she was so close. Just a bit farther.

It wasn't a campfire. It was light shining through a window.

A cabin. A small, crude cabin, a window beside the front door flickering orange, inviting, welcoming.

A horse stood in a fenced-in corral, watching her approach. Its ears were up and it stamped its hooves nervously.

The door to the cabin swung open and Walker stepped out, holding a rifle, glancing left and right. He wore dark pants and an untucked, unbuttoned white shirt. He saw Katherine and lowered the rifle.

"How'd you find me?" he asked. He didn't seem surprised to see her. Not angry. Almost like he'd been expecting her.

"I'm not sure," she said, shaking her head. "I couldn't sleep. I saw the light, and I just went toward it."

He leaned the rifle against the front of the cabin. "How did you know it wasn't Indians?"

Her brow furrowed as she thought about it. "I didn't. I just

25

knew, somehow, that this was where I should go." She moved closer to him. If she wanted, she could reach out and touch him. She wanted to.

He nodded. "And here you are."

She stepped forward and put a hand on his chest. "And here I am." He was so warm, so alive. She smiled up at him. Her hand, as if of its own accord, slid up over his chest and caressed his cheek. "So, what now?" she asked. "Should I go back?"

"Do you want to?" he said.

"No," she replied.

He turned his head and kissed her palm, took it in his own, and pulled her close. Her breasts pressed up against his chest. His lips were soft, but firm at the same time, as he kissed her. No one had ever kissed her like this. Certainly not Thomas.

Walker's kisses were tender at first, then more forceful. And she kissed him right back.

At some point they made it inside the cabin, where they made love on a fur rug in front of the fireplace. He was gentle and caring, his hands and lips exploring her body. She felt sensations she had never felt before, reached heights never dreamed of. Was this what it was supposed to be like?

Afterward, they spoke softly, Katherine telling him of her baby girl, without shame, only sorrow.

He had lost his wife many years ago, he said, and, like her, had headed West to start over. His sons had died of dysentery, not Indians. He hadn't the heart to go on, he told her. What was the point? He stayed here. He had a nice life, he said.

They made love a second time, slow and languid, only this time, Katherine took charge. He had emboldened her, somehow. She climbed atop him, and as he moved beneath her, she bent down and kissed him.

They fell asleep entangled in each other's arms and legs.

* * *

She awoke, not knowing where she was, and looked around. Walker lay beside her, breathing softly. How had she wound up here, she wondered? Not upset at herself, not angry. Just... at peace. Comfortable, but a little cold. The fire was out, and the only light came through the front window. Morning.

He stirred beside her and opened his eyes, blinked, and smiled at her. "You're still here."

She sat up, pulling the blanket to cover herself. "Should I go?"

He looked at her. Really looked at her. He smiled and put his hand on her bare shoulder. "Do you want to leave?"

"No." It was out before she had time to think.

He nodded. "Good."

She grinned back at him, dropped the blanket, pulled his hand from her shoulder down to her breast. "You know, some people think you're a ghost."

He shook his head, looking a little wistful. "I'm not the ghost," he said. "You are."

"What?" Her smile faltered, and a wave of cold swept over her. "What do you mean?"

He didn't reply. Just kept looking at her. Those green eyes, probing her. Wanting her to figure out what he meant. She pulled away from him and covered herself with the blanket. She stared at him, asking without asking. What did he mean?

He nodded, encouraging her. *You got this.*

Katherine's mind raced. Images and memories. *Her daughter born dead. The woman looking down, then leaving her. A rough-hewn cross atop a tiny mound of dirt planted beside a wagon trail... waking up, alone, in the dark... alone in the dark....*

She gasped, struggling to make sense of this. Tears obscured her vision and she wiped her eyes and looked at Walker. "I... I don't understand... I died...?"

He nodded, took her in his arms. "It's all right. This is a good place. You can stay with me," he said. "With us."

A peal of childish laughter from outside. A shout.

She turned to the front door and stood up.

"My sons," he said. "They visit me. That's why I couldn't leave."

Katherine looked around, found her dress in a heap beside the door, and pulled it over her head. She opened the door and looked outside. The morning was beautiful, bright and full of promise.

Two young boys climbing on the corral fence turned to her and smiled. The younger one waved. She looked around. A small vegetable garden, lush and green. Chickens clawing at the dirt by her feet. A creek off to the side of the house. It was beautiful. It was perfect.

Walker stepped out beside her.

The boys saw him. "Papa!" the little one cried and they both dropped from the fence and ran to him. He grabbed the two of them in a bear hug, kissing the tops of their heads as they giggled and squirmed. He released them, and they raced to the creek.

"There's another reason you should stay here," he said.

"What's that?" she asked.

He stepped back inside the front door and motioned for her to follow. She glided past him and looked to the bed. A baby lay upon it. A little squirming baby. Katherine put her hands up to her mouth, strode across the room, and picked up her daughter.

3

THE STAGECOACH TO BADGER'S GULCH

Deborah Grahl

Chapter One

Wyoming, 1888

A gentle breeze stirred the tall prairie grass that stretched north to the Platte River. The sun shone in a clear sky as the stagecoach bounced and rattled over the dusty road from Cheyenne to the small town of Badger's Gulch. Cassandra Prescott, uncomfortable from the heat inside the coach and the hard seat, wished she could conjure a nice soft pillow to sit on. Her mouth formed a grim line. This entire situation was too vexing to be believed—banished to the wilds of Wyoming because a few ladies of the church auxiliary dropped by unexpectedly and saw the cherry pie she had baked float across the room to land on the windowsill. What was she supposed to have done? Her hands were covered with flour, and the first pie needed to cool.

Cassandra gnawed her bottom lip. And there was the spoon in the mixing bowl stirring the pie filling, by itself. *Damn it anyway.* Those women were dreadful and had no business spying on her. Her two sisters, Anuria and Belinda, had tried to convince them they really hadn't seen a pie fly or a spoon spin, but to no avail.

Witches weren't being burned or hanged in Salem anymore, but

29

after speaking to her sisters and the coven, it had been decided that it would be for the best if Cassandra went to live with her Aunt Prudence, who had years earlier been banished for selling her erotic herbal elixir to the ladies of Salem. At the memory of Judge Parker's wife chasing him around his courtroom, Cassandra placed a gloved hand over her mouth and stifleding a laugh. Now here she was off to help Aunt Prudence train a small group of young witches.

Sighing, Cassandra surreptitiously studied the coach's only other occupant, a cowboy seated across from her, who, as far as Cassandra could tell, had been asleep since the stage pulled out of Cheyenne. She peered closer. Even though he was in need of a shave, he certainly was handsome. She couldn't tell what color his eyes were, but his lashes were thick, and they rested on high cheek bones. His nose was straight and his lips full. Under his hat, his hair was dark blond and slightly too long. His clothes were somewhat wrinkled, but looked clean. He seemed well built with wide shoulders and long legs which happened to be stretched out, his booted feet propped on the seat next to her.

Cassandra tugged at the collar of her dove-gray traveling dress. The coach was stifling. She concealed her hand between the folds of her dress, wiggled her fingers, and produced a gray and white pleated fan. As she cooled herself, she was about to throw caution to the wind and produce a pillow when her companion's eyes opened and met hers.

Cassandra's breath caught. Cornflower blue was the only description she could think of for his incredible eyes. Handsome was right. *Oh, my,* she thought as she tried to gather her wits. She smiled. "Good morning."

He nodded. "Ma'am." He yawned, stretched, and set his feet on the floor. "Where are we?" His voice was husky with a slight southern drawl.

Cassandra shook her head. "I have no idea. I was told that with one overnight stop we'd make Badger's Gulch by tomorrow morning, but as slow as we're going, I doubt that."

He smiled, showing straight white teeth. "If we don't have any trouble, we should make it."

"Trouble? Such as?"

He shrugged. "The stage could break down; one of the horses could come up lame; we could be attacked by Indians, or held up by outlaws."

At thoughts of Indians and outlaws, the motion of Cassandra's fan abruptly stopped, and all discomfort of her sore backside fled. Her eyes opened wide. "Are you serious?"

Seeing the horrified expression on her pretty face, Reece silently swore. The chance of any of those things actually happening was pretty slim, but for some reason he hadn't been able to restrain himself. He sighed. He knew exactly what was wrong with him, and he'd taken his edginess out on her.

Reece grinned to put her at ease. "I'm sure we'll reach Badger's Gulch without any problems. By the way, I'm Reece McGraw."

"Cassandra Prescott. How do you do?"

Reece tipped his hat. "Ma'am. By your accent, I'd guess you're from back Eeast."

"Salem, Massachusetts."

"That's quite a ways from here. What brings you out Wwest?"

"I have an aunt in Badger's Gulch, and I'm going to help her teach…" She hesitated. "… in a school she's begun."

Cassandra Prescott didn't look like any school teacher Reece had ever met. She was a real beauty with dark red hair beneath a gray and white straw hat, clear green eyes, a slightly turned-up nose, perfectly sculpted lips, all set in a heart-shaped face, and, if he was any judge, had a very nice figure under those clothes.

"How about you?" she asked. "What takes you to Badger's Gulch?"

Reece cleared his throat. Until she'd told him, he'd had no idea where the stage was going. "I have business in town." The truth was that an outlaw gang was after him for killing their leader during a train robbery. Reece's older brother, a Deputy Marshal, had been mortally shot. The U.S. Marshals knew Reece had killed in self-defense, but the remaining outlaws had gotten away and were trailing him. After riding all night, he'd climbed into the first stage leaving Cheyenne. He planned on laying low, hoping the Marshals could round up the gang.

Reece glanced out the windows on either side of him. The prairie stretched for miles to the horizon, and other than a few trees, visibility was good. He should be able to see any riders coming behind them.

"Are you looking for someone?" Cassandra asked.

He quickly turned his attention back to Cassandra. He needed to keep his unease under control. He believed he'd covered his trail, and that the gang didn't know where he was. All he had to do now was make it to Badger's Gulch.

Reece shook his head. "No, ma'am, just watching the scenery go by."

Cassandra frowned. "Mr. McGraw, please don't call me ma'am. Considering I'm twenty-two years old, it makes me feel like someone's grandmother."

Reece's lips twitched. "Miss Prescott, I can assure you that you don't look like anyone's grandmother."

Cassandra smiled. "I'm glad to hear it."

"Tell me, why is it that such an attractive young woman is traveling alone? Is there a Mr. Prescott?"

She arched one brow.

He inwardly chided himself. Why had he asked her that? "Sorry, it's none of my business."

Amusement filled her eyes. "No, Mr. McGraw, I'm not married." She frowned. "It seems we're stopping. Do you think there's a problem?"

Reece leaned forward and peered out the window. "We're probably stopping to change horses and have a lunch break."

Chapter Two

As a two-story log structure came into view, Cassandra sighed with relief. Her stomach had been growling for miles, and she desperately needed to relieve herself.

"Do you think we'll be here for very long?" she asked as Reece helped her from the coach.

"No more than thirty minutes, ma'am," the coach driver replied before Reece could answer. "You can get something to eat and anything else you need inside. Mae and Walter Porter will take good care of you."

Cassandra hurried toward the inn's front door and was greeted by a friendly tall woman with a lined face and dull blondeblond hair.

"Howdy," she said with a smile, showing crooked front teeth. "Come on in and set yourself down. I've got some hot rabbit stew and warm fresh bread."

Cassandra tried to hide her chagrin. Rabbit stew was not among

32

her favorite foods. She smiled back. "It sounds delicious, but I'm not all that hungry. Could I just have some of the bread, perhaps with butter? And coffee?"

Mae nodded. "Sure thing." She peered around Cassandra. "Are you traveling alone?"

"No, there's one other." Cassandra lowered her voice. "I need to use the…

Before she could finish, Mae pointed. "Privy is out back, down that hall and through the door."

Cassandra sighed. In Salem, her home had indoor plumbing with wonderful flush commodes. Reluctantly she made her way to the back of the inn and headed toward the wooden structure. Finishing her business, she was about to open the door when a commotion outside made her hesitate. The privy door was jerked open, and Reece pulled her out.

"Mr. McGraw, what are you doing?" Cassandra cried.

"You have to get back inside the cabin right away," he insisted as he abruptly hauled her across the yard past a vegetable garden, the chicken coop, and a lean-to full of stacked wood.

"Mr. McGraw, what is the matter with you?" Cassandra shouted, as she tried to pull her arm from his grip.

Not slowing their pace, he ignored her question and her efforts to break free practically carrying her up the steps onto the porch. Once inside the inn, he released her, slammed the door behind them, and dropped the iron bar across the latch.

Quivering with outrage, Cassandra glowered at Reece and asked, "Mr. McGraw, would you like to explain your despicable conduct?"

In two strides, Reece was standing in front of her nose-to-nose as he growled, "What my 'despicable conduct' just did, was save you from being captured or killed by outlaws. So, for the rest of our time together, I suggest you do as I say."

Shock filled her eyes as she stepped back and took in her surroundings. In the long low room that ran along the front of the cabin, both the Porter's knelt near the windows and held guns. Outside, she could hear muffled sounds of men shouting. She turned to Reece, who was loading bullets into another rifle.

"Mr. McGraw, what's happening?" she asked.

Reece glanced at her stricken face and cursed. As soon as he'd seen the men coming, he should have jumped on a horse and ridden away, but there hadn't been time. The outlaws had already shot the coach driver, and all Reece could think of was finding Cassandra and getting her to safety. "They're looking for me. I'm sorry I led them here, but I honestly thought they didn't know where I'd gone."

Cassandra narrowed her eyes. "Why are they after you? Are you also an outlaw?"

"No. They want me because I killed their leader after he killed my brother during a train robbery."

"There are only five of them," Walter Porter said. "I'm a decent shot with the Sharps, and Mae's got the double-barreled twelve-gauge. With your Winchester, we can beat them."

"We need to watch out back," Mae said.

Cassandra gnawed on her lower lip. When she'd left Salem, she had been told that under no circumstances, until she arrived at her Aunt Prudence's house, was she to use her powers. But they needed her help. She cleared her throat. "I can watch."

The three turned to stare at her. Reece was the first to speak. "That's nice of you to offer, but these are dangerous outlaws, and we need someone who can shoot to keep an eye on the back."

Cassandra's spine stiffened. If it had been left to her, the outlaws would already be bound and gagged and the rest of them would be having their rabbit stew. She balled her hands into fists in absolute frustration. Closing her eyes, she recited a calming spell. When she felt she could address Reece McGraw without wanting to turn him into a toad, she replied, "Trust me, Mr. McGraw, I'm perfectly capable of watching the yard for outlaws."

Before Reece could reply, a man's voice shouted from out front. "Send out McGraw, and we'll leave the rest of you in peace."

Reece's mouth formed a thin line. He already had the coach driver's death on his hands. He couldn't put the others in danger. "I'll go." He laid down his rifle.

"No," Cassandra shouted. "They'll kill you."

"She's right," Walter said. "We don't give in to outlaws. Pick your rifle up, son, and let's get 'em."

Reece took his place on the opposite side of the door from Walter and Mae. "If I see one of them move toward the back, I'll head that way."

"I'll count to ten, and if you haven't sent McGraw out, we'll start shooting," the leader shouted.

As he counted, Cassandra slowly made her way toward the back of the cabin. When she heard the bullets begin to thud into the logs and a window shatter, she eased the iron bar from the door and stepped outside. Carefully, she made her way around the side of the cabin until the riders came into view. Concentrating on the first man, she flung up her arm and his rifle flew from his hands. She quickly waved her hand and he fell to the ground. The other outlaws, assuming he had been shot, didn't notice the rope that appeared and, on its own, tied him up.

Those in the house were now returning fire, and a second outlaw went down, this one with a .52 caliber hole in his chest. Cassandra, turning her attention to the third man, repeated her ministrations until he also lay tied and gagged.

The two still on their horses turned and noticed the men lying on the ground. "What the hell?" tThe one closer to Cassandra shouted.

As Cassandra raised her hand to bring him down, he spotted her. Giving her an evil smile, he aimed his pistol toward her. Before he could fire, Cassandra's arm swung up and his gun leaped from his hand.

Shock and confusion filled his face. He said something to his companion, who also looked her way. Abruptly, they turned their horses to where their fellow outlaws lay, threw them across their saddles and led them away.

Cassandra, smiling with satisfaction, made her way around the side of the cabin, only to walk directly into Reece.

"What the hell do you think you're doing?" he asked through gritted teeth.

Damn, she thought, *had he seen her perform magic?* Deciding to test the waters, she innocently asked, "What do you mean?"

"I mean that after I told you to stay inside, you come out here and take a chance of being either shot or kidnapped." He leaned forward. "Did you not hear the exchange of gunfire?"

His mouth being so close to hers, all thoughts of outlaws fled Cassandra's mind. A giddy sensation filled her. *What if he kisses me?* The thought of this had her licking suddenly dry lips. She stared into his eyes watching them change from anger to… desire? Cassandra swallowed hard. Waiting in anticipation, she blinked in disappointment as he abruptly stepped back.

A strange expression came over his face before he gruffly asked, "Would you like to explain why you ignored me?"

It took her a moment to get her thoughts away from imagined kisses back to outlaws. She was relieved he hadn't seen the men she'd taken down. She smiled. "I wanted to help." She pulled her hand from behind her back and showed him the derringer she held.

Reece snorted. "What the hell did you think you were going to do with that toy?"

Cassandra frowned. *The ungrateful wretch. If it hadn't been for me, they might all be dead.* And she couldn't say a word to defend herself. To her utter humiliation, her eyes began to fill with frustrated tears. Misunderstanding the source, Reece's voice softened.

"It's okay, please don't cry. I know you only wanted to help." He took her by the arm. "Come on, let's go back inside."

When they reentered the cabin, Walter was already nailing a board across the broken window. "I'm surprised they turned tail like that, but I'm afraid they'll be back."

Reece nodded. "As soon as we get the windows secure and bury the coach driver, I'll leave. I don't want to put your lives in any further danger."

Mae, who had swept up the broken glass, gave Cassandra a wary glance.

Damn, Cassandra thought. She must have seen me. Deciding to act as if nothing had happened, she approached the older woman. "Mae, can I help?"

Mae shook her head and took a step back.

Inwardly sighing, Cassandra lowered her voice. "Is there something wrong?"

Mae waited until Reece and Walter headed out the front door before answering. "I don't know what you are or how you did what you did, but when Reece leaves, I want you to go with him."

"Certainly, I'll go, but I mean you no harm."

"I don't believe you do. I've lived long enough out on this prairie to have seen some strange happenings. All I know is that I am a God-fearing woman and I want no part of whatever you are. Now, Reece is going to insist you wait for the next stage. You need to convince him to take you with him."

Cassandra nodded. "I understand."

"You can take a horse, and I'll fix you some food for your

journey."

Chapter Three

If only I could wave my hand and transport us to Badger's Gulch,
Cassandra thought as she sat on the horse and held onto Reece.
She'd had to threaten to set out on her own to get Reece to agree to
take her with him. Now here they were in the middle of nowhere,
and it would be getting dark. "Do you think we'll stop soon?" she
hesitantly asked.

"If you think we'll come across a grand hotel, Miss Prescott,
you're going to be highly disappointed," came his gruff reply. "As
soon as I find a spot I feel is secure, we'll make camp."

Cassandra gnawed on her bottom lip. Her powers were limited,
but if she tried hard enough, she might be able to produce some kind
of shelter. She closed her eyes and with all her concentration
projected her power forward.

"Well, I'll be damned," Reece said as they rounded a grove of
trees and saw a small barn in the distance.

Cassandra let out a sigh of relief. The barn looked a little rickety,
but for her first attempt at conjuring something that large, it wasn't
too bad. "Perhaps we can stay there," she tentatively suggested.

"Perhaps," he murmured, as he stopped in front of the barn.
"There's nothing around here for miles. What is a barn doing here?"

"Oh, what does it matter?" Cassandra replied as she slid from
the horse. "It looks safe and dry."

"Wait a minute," Reece called as he dismounted. "Let me check
inside before you go walking into a trap."

Cassandra peered over his shoulder as he eased open the door.
She smiled to herself as she heard his intake of breath. She may have
gone overboard, but she wasn't about to sleep on the cold ground
without clean straw and blankets. Nor sit in the dark without a
lantern.

Reece turned and with a puzzled expression, held the door open
for her to pass.

"I think this will do nicely," she said, taking in her handiwork.

Reece frowned. "Don't you find this a little peculiar? There's
nothing around us for miles, but here's a clean unoccupied barn with
all the provisions we'll need. Where's the house?"

Cassandra shrugged. "Who knows, maybe they had to leave and

37

all they had time to build was this barn." She headed back out the door. "Or the house burned down, and they were all murdered by Indians. The point is that we have food and shelter. While you take care of the horse and bring in our supplies, I'm going for a walk."

Heading into the trees, she made sure Reece couldn't see her. She conjured a nice chamber pot, did her business, made the pot disappear, and reentered the barn as Reece was unpacking their saddlebagssaddle bags. She sat on a bale of hay. "I'm starving., Wwhat did Mae pack for us?"

"There's cured bacon and canned beans." He placed the food on a tin plate and handed it to her. "You'll have to eat it cold. We can't take a chance of someone seeing the smoke from a fire."

As their hands touched, a thrill of excitement tingled through Cassandra. When she looked into his eyes, his expression told her he'd felt it as well. Whatever had passed between them had nothing to do with magic, but certainly was just as powerful.

What the hell had just happened? Reece thought as he chewed his food and studied Cassandra. Even though he was attracted to her, there was something about her that made him uneasy. Besides, the last thing he needed was to get involved with Cassandra Prescott.

"Tell me about yourself, Mr. McGraw," Cassandra said, interrupting his thoughts.

"What would you like to know?"

"Well, where are you from?"

"Denver."

"Are you married?"

"Nope."

"What do you do to make a living?"

"I own a cattle ranch."

At his clipped response, Cassandra's mouth formed a thin line. "Mr. McGraw, if you don't wish to converse with me, or choose to keep your personal life to yourself, please just say so."

I'd rather kiss you senseless and make love to you for hours. Whoa, cowboy, where did that thought come from? He cleared his throat. "I'm just tired. Perhaps we should get some sleep."

She nodded, but neither moved. They sat staring into each other's eyes.

Cassandra looked to where blankets lay upon a mound of straw and her cheeks turned pink. "There seems to be only one bed."

Again their eyes met. A voice in Reece's head was telling him to keep his distance. Ignoring this, he reached out his hand. In a low voice, he said, "Lay with me."

Cassandra hesitated. She knew propriety dictated she should tell him no, but she'd been attracted to him since he'd looked at her with his incredible blue eyes. She was twenty-two and still a virgin. Some would consider her an old maid. The promise in his eyes and her own need had her damning propriety and reaching out her hand.

They fell onto the bed of straw and his lips covered hers. When their tongues met, Cassandra moaned and pressed closer to him. His hand slowly explored her body, flaming the desire building inside her.

"I want to make love to you," Reece whispered.

"Oh, yes," Cassandra replied.

Reece began to unbutton the front of her dress, revealing her camisole and corset. Women wear too many damn clothes," he muttered as he removed her camisole and began to unhook her corset. When he exposed her firm round breasts, Reece smiled. "You're beautiful." He lowered his head and took one pink-tipped nipple into his mouth.

Not knowing what to expect, Cassandra gasped with pleasure as he sucked and licked until her nipples were plump with need. "Oh, my, that's very nice."

Reece's head came up, and the heat in his eyes sent a thrill coursing through her body.

"I'm glad you like it. Let's get you out of these clothes, and I'll show you something I think you'll like even more."

Cassandra soon found herself naked in front of a total stranger. It was a little uncomfortable watching his eyes rove over her, but when he smiled and bent his head to kiss her, she knew giving herself to this man was exactly what she wanted to do.

As he kissed her, his hand moved across her breast, down her side and over her hip. Cassandra stiffened when he touched her inner thigh then the junction between her legs.

"Relax, darlin," he whispered. "Let me touch you."

The desire that shot through Cassandra when his fingers began to stroke her took her breath away. She couldn't help but groan aloud when his thumb moved over her swollen bud. "Reece, something is happening," she panted.

"Let it come, darlin,"

39

When he slid two fingers into her and began to move them in and out, Cassandra cried aloud as her climax rippled throughout her body.

Reece watched the pleasure on her beautiful face, and his own need for her threatened to make him lose all self-control. "That's it, darlin, let it come."

"Reece, oh, sweet heaven," Cassandra cried.

"We're not there yet, but soon," Reece said, his voice low and husky. He quickly removed his clothes and spread her legs.

He saw the look of unease as she stared at his swollen manhood.

"Reece, I don't know if this is going to work."

Reece grinned. "Trust me. It will work." He lowered his head for another long-heated kiss, then positioned himself to enter her. She was hot and wet and ready for him, but he knew he had to go easy. He slowly slid into her, watching her face for any discomfort. He felt her tense when he reached her virginity. "Relax, Cassandra, let me in." He once again kissed her as he thrust hard, breaking the barrier of her womanhood.

She cried out, but soon was moving with him. Reece felt her nails digging into his back as his thrusts became more demanding. "God, darlin', you're sweet," he whispered. "I want to feel you come. Christ!," he shouted as she screamed his name, and his own release crashed through him.

The magic that flowed through Cassandra's veins had never given her the exhilaration Reece had when he'd entered her. Now as she lay in his arms, their legs intertwined, she sighed with contentment.

Reece kissed her tenderly. "Are you alrightall right?"

Cassandra smiled. "I've never been better."

Reece smiled back. "Me too."

Cassandra sighed. "No one ever told me how thrilling love-making can be."

Reece stroked her breast. "So you found it thrilling, did you?"

"Oh, yes."

As he nuzzled her neck, Reece's hand moved between her legs. "Are you up to more thrills?"

Instantly, Cassandra's body responded to his touch. Feeling reckless she reached down and wrapped her hand around his already hard erection. "Oh, yes, cowboy, I'm ready."

Chapter Four

Cassandra couldn't breathe without choking. She opened her eyes and saw nothing but gray smoke. Gasping for breath, she sat up and saw the flames blocking the barn door. She reached for Reece.

"Reece, wake up." When he didn't answer, panic threatened to overcome her.

She tossed off the blanket, waved her hand, and they were both dressed. She tied a scarf over her mouth and knelt next to Reece and shook him as hard as she could. When he didn't respond, she again waved her hand. The blanket raised him off the floor. The effect of the smoke was weakening her and her powers. Her eyes streaming, lungs aching, she pulled him toward the back of the barn. It took her three tries before her powers were strong enough for her to make an opening in the boards and drag Reece out.

Weak, lightheaded and gagging, Cassandra collapsed next to him. Everything went dark.

"Hello, witch woman" was the next thing she heard.

She was laying on her back, her hands and feet bound. She tried to see where Reece was, but her view was blocked by two outlaws holding guns.

"Your boyfriend isn't doing too well," the outlaw next to her sneered. "Think he might have had too much smoke."

Remembered pleasure of the night before came rushing back. Then anger took its place. How dare these outlaws taint the most wonderful night of her life?. Still feeling weak and sick, Cassandra tried to speak, but her throat was too raw. She desperately tried to regain her full power.

What's the matter, witch woman, cat got your tongue?" The outlaws laughed.

"What have you done with Reece?" she croaked.

"We ain't done nothin' yet. Your boyfriend's life is going to determine on how well you do as I say." The one who spoke had dirty-blond hair and a scar over his eye. "I'm thinking with your power, you can conjure us up lots of money."

"Yeah, like a big pile of gold eagles." This outlaw had a scraggly beard and cold blue eyes.

Cassandra narrowed her eyes in outrage. In a voice barely above a whisper, she said, "You ignorant buffoon, I can't conjure gold or money."

"Hey, Clawson, if the witch doesn't do as you ask, we can torture McGraw until she does," an outlaw with a missing front tooth suggested.

Clawson scratched his chin. "Buster, I was kind of thinkin' the same thing. If she doesn't do as we say and tries to hurt us, we'll kill her cowboy. Or maybe just shoot his pecker off." He grinned showing brown crooked teeth. "Snake, you and Buster make sure McGraw is tied up real good and put him where the witch can see him."

Cassandra tried to sit up. If she could free one of her hands, she could strike them down.

Clawson's gun cocked. "Don't move, witch. You stay flat on your back. I figure as long as your hands are underneath you, we're safe."

Cassandra smiled. "Are you foolish enough to think my powers are only in my hands?"

Clawson looked uneasy, while the other two stepped back.

Cassandra played to her advantage. Her power *was* only in her hands, but they didn't know that. If she could wiggle her fingers and make something move, it might scare them into leaving. A rock near Clawson's foot would work. She concentrated and was able to move two fingers. The rock leaped in the air and hit Clawson on the knee.

"Damn it," he swore and jumped back. He glowered at her. "You want to play games? Snake, shoot McGraw in the foot."

To Cassandra's horror, the man aimed his gun. "No, stop," she cried. She turned her head to see Reece, face down, his hands and feet tied. Cassandra couldn't tell if he was dead or alive. "Have you already killed him?"

"Nope. He's still alive."

"He needs medical attention," Cassandra shouted.

Clawson looked from her to Reece and nodded. "I'd say he does. So, if you want to save him, produce our gold coins, and we'll let you two go."

Their satisfied smirks told Cassandra they had no intention of letting them go. She swallowed back her fear. She must outwit them. "How do you expect for me to do anything when I can't use my hands?"

"I've considered that conundrum, and the only solution I came up with is for Snake to have a gun at McGraw's head. If you make a move to hurt any of us, he shoots."

Cassandra bit her lower lip. She could probably take down two of them, but not all three. But she could do nothing as she was. She nodded. "Let me up and untie me."

Clawson motioned for Snake to prop McGraw against a tree while Burt untied Cassandra.

Burt cautiously approached her. Cassandra smiled, but she knew her hatred glowed in her eyes.

"You hurt me, witch, and McGraw dies," Burt stammered.

Cassandra rolled onto her side and Burt quickly sliced through her ropes.

"Leave her feet tied," Clawson said. "We don't want her running away."

"What if she can fly?," Snake asked.

Cassandra couldn't stop herself. She rose to her knees and flapped her arms. All three men shouted, and Snake's gun went off.

Everyone went still. Reece lay on his side, blood staining the top of his leg.

"Reece," Cassandra cried and tried to hobble to him.

"Don't move, witch," Clawson said. "Snake, is he dead?"

"Nah. My hand jerked, and the bullet grazed his leg. He'll bleed, but it will take a while for him to bleed out."

Cassandra shook uncontrollably. How could she have pulled such an idiotic stunt? If Reece dieds it would be her fault.

"One more bullet will do your boyfriend in," Clawson said. I suggest you produce our gold."

Cassandra gritted her teeth. "How was she to convince these men that she couldn't do as they asked. "I told you, I can't conjure anything used as currency."

Clawson fired. The bullet inches from where Reece lay.

Cassandra silently prayed to all the goddesses for help. Certainly she could outwit these evil men.

"Time's running out. The flames from the barn are only embers now, but the smoke might attract someone. We need our gold."

Inspiration dawned on Cassandra. She couldn't produce real gold, but she could conjure fake coins. But would they be fooled? She only needed enough time to get to Reece and free him. She took a deep breath. "All right, I'm going to wave my hand and give you your gold. If you shoot Reece, I may not be able to get all of you… "

she glared at each outlaw. "But I'll get at least one."

The men nodded, but visibly tensed. Snake pressed his gun against Reece's head.

"No funny business, or he dies," Clawson said.

"I'll need to stand," Cassandra said. "You're going to have to untie my feet."

Clawson nodded to Burt who warily approached Cassandra. As quickly as possible, he slit the ropes and she stood.

Just then Reece opened his eyes. His face soot-streaked, blood soaking his pants, Cassandra still thought he was the handsomest man she'd ever seen.

"What the hell is going on?" Reese rasped.

"The witch is about to make us rich men," Clawson stated. "So you stay nice and quiet, or Snake might accidently blow your brains out."

Reece narrowed his eyes. "Witch? What are you talking about?"

Clawson gestured to Cassandra. "Your girlfriend. You see, if she doesn't give us the gold coins, Snake's going to kill you."

"Clawson, you've been smokin' too much loco weed. Cassandra is not a witch, and she certainly can't produce gold coins."

Clawson snorted. "Is that right? Tell that to my men the witch took down."

Reece tried to rise. "It's me you want, not her."

Snake cocked his gun. "Move another inch, and you're a dead man."

"Maybe we should just kill them and get out of here," Burt said.

Clawson shook his head. "I'm not leavin' without the gold." He turned to Cassandra. "All right, witch, time's up. Give me the gold."

Cassandra glanced to where Reece sat. Confusion filled his face. If only she had time to explain. What will he think of her when he sees her perform magic? She gave him what she hoped was a reassuring smile and waved her hand. Sacks of gold coins appeared at the feet of each outlaw.

"Yippee!" Burt and Snake yelled as they gathered the bags.

Reece's eyes opened wide, then narrowed. The confusion in their blue depths made her heart sink. She'd seen it before. People looked at someone like her as if she belonged in a freak show.

"Not so fast," Clawson said. "Give me one of those bags. I want to make sure she's not trying to cheat us."

Cassandra held her breath. *Please let them be fooled by the fake gold.*

Clawson opened one bag and pulled out a handful of gold coins. He studied them, frowned, then stared at Cassandra.

Had she not put the correct images on the coins? If her recollection was correct, the American eagle was on one side and Lady Liberty on the other.

Clawson smiled. "You know, witch, you might be a good person to keep around. Me and the boys wouldn't have to rob anymore trains or banks. You could give us anything we wanted."

Real fear dampened Cassandra's palms. Could the wretchedretched man honestly be considering taking her with him? And what would he do when he discovered the coins were fake? Oh, how she wished she could take him down where he stood.

Chapter Five

Incredulous, Reece sat trying to take in the scene in front of him. His lungs ached and his leg hurt like hell. He glanced at what was left of the barn. The last thing he remembered was falling asleep with Cassandra in his arms. Memories of her beneath him tugged at his heart. *Did I spend the night making love to a witch? That's crazy.* But he couldn't deny what he'd just seen.

He looked down at his bloodstained pants and back at Cassandra. When he'd fallen asleep, he'd been naked. Had she had time to dress him before they escaped from the barn? And how had she gotten them both out? The outlaws were paying more attention to the gold than him. If he could untie his hands, he could perhaps get to the knife he kept in his boot.

Clawson was scratching his beard stubble. "If I take you with me, witch, I'm gonna have to figure out how to keep you from hurting me and the boys."

Cassandra balled her hands into fists. "I'll go nowhere with you."

"Well, if you don't want us to kill McGraw, I don't see that you have much choice."

Reece, watching Cassandra, saw her fingers move and felt the ropes around his hands and ankles loosen. Then he felt something hard between him and the tree. As he watched, flames shot from the middle of the barn's embers. All three outlaws stood staring. Reece didn't waste any time. He reached behind him and grabbed the gun. Pain shot through his leg as he stumbled to his feet.

"Don't move," he growled, as he pressed the gun to Snake's back.

In one sweeping motion, Cassandra waved her arm and knocked Clawson and Burt to the ground. Another sweep of her hand and their arms and legs were tied. "You odious men. You will remain as you are until the U.S. Marshals arrive to take you to jail where you belong."

Still with his gun to Snake's back, in a low husky voice Reece asked. "What the hell are you?"

"She's some kind of demon," Clawson cried. "We couldn't even kill her with fire."

Cassandra glowered at Clawson. "I'm no demon." She turned to Reece. "I'm, um, well, a witch." When he only stared, she quickly continued. "But I'm a good witch." She frowned. "Well, most of the time." When Reece frowned, she hurried on. "It's true. I'm not like those illustrations of hags flying around on brooms." Her voice cracked. "Reece, please, don't judge me."

Reece's mind drifted back in time to the small band of Cherokee he'd come upon in Oklahoma. A medicine woman had come up to him, touched his arm, and said, "Trust the green-eyed woman. She has strong magic. She will bring you love."

Before Reece realized what was happening, Snake fired his gun and Cassandra cried out as she fell to her knees. With blood staining the side of her dress, she managed to wiggle her fingers and Snake went down.

Reece cursed. How could he have taken his attention off Snake. Cassandra lay clutching her side. "You son-of-a-bitch," Reece snarled as he tied Snake's hands and feet. "If she dies, I won't wait until the marshals get here, I'll blow your goddamned head off."

Reece, hurried to Cassandra, knelt and took her into his arms. "How bad are you hurt?"

"I don't know," she whispered.

Panic clawed at Reece's chest. Witch or not, he didn't want to lose her. "Can you heal yourself?"

"No. I need my aunt in Badger's Gulch."

Reece could see the pain in her eyes and hear it in her voice. "I've got to try and stop the bleeding. I have to see the wound."

Cassandra feebly waved her hand and they were inside a tent. "Now those awful men can't see."

Reece cocked his head. "Did you make the barn appear?"

She nodded. "I'm truly a good witch."

"Can you make yourself clothes?"

"Yes."

He reached down and tore her blood-stained dress and frowned. The bullet had sliced deep across her side. "I'm going to need bandages."

"I'll try. Reece, I never meant to deceive you."

"I know." She looked as if she was about to pass out.

"Cassandra, the bandages."

Feebly she moved her fingers and white cloth appeared.

As gently as possible, Reece wrapped the strips around her waist. "I'll be right back." He collected the outlaws' guns and lifted Cassandra into his arms.

"Reece, your leg," Cassandra murmured.

"I'll be fine."

He headed for the horses. "This is going to hurt like hell, but we're going to have to ride."

"Hey, McGraw, where the hell are you goin'?" Clawson called. "You can't leave us here like this."

"The hell I can't," Reece replied. "The marshals will eventually find you."

Reece sat Cassandra on the grass and untied the horses. Seeing the pain in her eyes, he kissed her pale lips. "I'm going to put you in my arms in front of me."

Cassandra nodded, then her eyelids closed.

Hours later, with a limp Cassandra in his arms, Reece rode into Badger's Gulch. Not knowing where her Aunt Prudence lived, he stopped the first person he saw, a young woman pruning a rose bush in her front yard. "Excuse me. I need to find a woman named Prudence. Can you help me?"

With wide eyes, she looked from him to Cassandra. He could imagine the sight they made. She nodded. "Miss Prudence lives at the other end of town in a white house with blue shutters."

Reece thanked her and nudged his horse forward. It didn't take long until he saw the house. With relief, he slid from the horse and carried Cassandra up the walk. His arms full of Cassandra, he kicked the door with his foot. The woman that answered was short and plump with silver hair and Cassandra's green eyes. She took one look

47

at them and motioned him in.

"Bring her this way," she said. "Tell me what happened, and after I take care of her, I'll see to your leg."

Reece carried Cassandra down a short hall and up the stairs. He followed Prudence into a sunny room and laid Cassandra on the bed. "She's been shot."

"Did you shoot her?"

"No. Some outlaws did."

"Is it your fault she got shot?" Prudence asked as she removed Cassandra's bandages.

His and Prudence's eyes met. "Yes," he replied. "Now you have to save her."

"You'd better hope I can." She motioned to the door. "Go downstairs and get yourself a drink. I'll let you know when I'm done."

* * *

A lovely floating sensation filled Cassandra. Voices came and went. Her mind drifted. Reece was kissing her. He was telling her to come back, that he loved her. She frowned. Back from where? She liked it right where she was, here in Reece's arms. The voices were getting louder. Her head began to pound. Reece's image was fading from her mind. Desperately she tried to bring him back. Her eyes fluttered open and she smiled. Reece was there. She reached out her hand and touched him. "Are you real?"

He smiled back. "Yep."

"Where are we?"

"Badger's Gulch."

"Aunt Prudence?"

"Right here." Prudence bustled into the room carrying a tray. "It's about time you woke up. You need to drink this broth so this young man can get some sleep. He insisted on staying by your side."

Cassandra's eyes met Reece's. "Thank you for getting me here. Please, don't feel as if you have to stay. My aunt will take good care of me."

Reece took her hand. "What if I want to stay?"

Cassandra blinked back tears. "You know what I am."

"I know you're beautiful and brave." He gave her a long kiss.

Prudence cleared her throat. "That's enough, cowboy. She's still

48

very weak and needs to drink this broth."

Cassandra blinked in confusion. "You don't mind that I'm a witch?"

"I have to admit it's a little disconcerting to know one's future wife is a witch, but I have my own idiosyncrasies."

Cassandra's heart soared. Had she heard him correctly? "Your future wife?"

"If you'll have me."

A smile spread across her face. "Oh, yes, cowboy, I'll have you."

He pressed his lips to hers and whispered. "I love you."

"I love you too," she whispered back.

Outside, the citizens of Badger's Gulch stared as a giant rainbow arched across a clear blue sky.

4

ONE GOOD DEED...

A Midnight Louie Tale

Carole Nelson Douglas

I woke up to a low growl and a chorus of coyotes in the distance. In the not-far-enough distance.

I sat up in a strange bed, an airy European feather coverlet barely brushing my goose bumps.

A sense of hot, canine panting tickled my left shoulder. This time the low growl was near my left ear.

Coyote yips and howls echoed off the house's stone exterior, walls too strong for any cousins of big bad wolves to blow them down, right?

I shook off the creepy, surrounded feeling. Nobody had written a fairy tale about a pack of hungry, howling coyotes taking down a house. Or a 21st-century woman having hallucinations in a strange bedroom.

My eyes focused on my only companion, the black cat whose green eyes reflected emergency-vehicle red from the window sill.

At least I wasn't alone in this desolate place. *Here, kitty, kitty.*

The cat's yawn revealed rows of tiny shark's teeth in a flash of lightning.

I didn't wait for housecat reinforcements, but rolled out of the high, old-fashioned bed, stubbing a toe on the nightstand brass leg—

Ouch! And felt in the dark for the small, high-intensity flashlight from my travel kit.

The wooden floor wasn't cold to my bare feet, a reminder I was visiting a warm, desert climate, even though it could turn bone-deep chilly during the night. The flashlight's narrow ray glinted off the beaded edges of the four-poster's lush crimson velvet draperies. I nearly jumped back into bed when the light reflected off the blue glass eyes of the wigged and corseted female dress form in the corner.

I ran the light over my guard cat, following the furry black form, lying from forepaws to haunches to final tail kink for what seemed like forever. The cat had merged with the dark to stretch out to the full length—not of the window sill, but of the corpse-long, bride's hope chest placed beneath it. *It was a huge black panther!*

Just then, something unseen and furred rolled off the bed against my hip. Below my knee-length sleep T-shirt, my calves and ankles were massaged by a hot, hairy form snaking to and fro. My tiny flashlight illuminated a trembling silken dust ruffle, but *nothing* was there!

Good thing I'd explored last night when I'd arrived… I tossed the flashlight on the featherbed and snatched the farmer's match box near the bedside oil lamp. The match-head clawed the striking surface with an owlish screech as the house-surrounding phenomenon of creature claws scratching the sturdy stone exterior amped up to max volume.

The wick caught flame. In the light of the oil lamp's glowing crimson globe, my giant cat of the dark was only a large domestic black cat, Midnight Louie by name, I'd been told. So back to bed.

And still the coyotes howled.

Welcome to Coyote Wells, Nevada, I told myself and the black cat, shivering under the covers of the massive bed. I thought back on how I got to this dark and scary place and vowed:

I, Lacey McIver, hope I am never so unlucky as to be a surprise heiress again.

* * *

"My great-uncle left me a business enterprise?" Lacey was mystified as she gazed at the lawyer across a mahogany desk the size of a pool table. "I hardly knew about him."

Lacey didn't get into downtown Los Angeles often. Just finding the law office among the skyscrapers was stressing to a small-town elementary school teacher from the Valley.

The waiting room had been filled with expensive leather chairs and silk flower arrangements, but luckily, few clients. Five minutes after arriving at Roberts and Roberts, Lacey was shown into an office with a window-wall view of adjacent towers.

She took a leather chair as the lawyer behind the desk greeted her and moved half-glasses from forehead to nose.

"Were you aware, Miss McIver, that you are the sole beneficiary of Hezekiah Caleb Smith?"

"I didn't even know great-uncle Heck was dead, although I'm not surprised. He must have been older than a redwood tree. I haven't seen him since I was four years old. He was a family legend, though. I'd heard he'd prospected for gold in the West as a young man."

So maybe he'd left her a gold mine? No such luck!

The lawyer shuffled the piled papers through her scarlet-nailed hands. Ms. Roberts was a chic silver-haired sixty-something wearing a designer suit worthy of Melania Trump's budget. "He found *something* valuable in this place, Miss McIver."

She slid legal-length papers over the acre of slick mahogany desktop. Lacey, short and hating it, dove forward to stop them spinning.

"A deed?" Lacey announced as she read the top line. "To 'Boots and Spurs'. What and where is it?"

"It's only four acres with a handful of outbuildings in the Mojave desert."

"Four acres in a desert? Where in the Mojave Desert?"

"South of Reno, Nevada, 'The biggest little city in the world' and in a region home to the Wild West's most colorful historical characters and hauntings. So I'd say your inheritance is a gold mine, all right."

Ms. Roberts wrote a figure with a lot of commas and spun it into Lacey's waiting hands. "Given what it makes a year."

"Two-point-two million dollars?" Lacey said.

"True, but puzzling for a Reno-friendly property half a state away from Nevada's notorious 'Sin City'. Far enough that the nearby land is mostly government owned."

"*Government* owned?"

Ms. Roberts arched thin black brows. "National parks, Sierra Mountains, as isolated as a major southern Nevada site called… 'Area 51'."

Oh my goodness. Visions of UFOs danced in Lacey's head as she eyed the figure before her. *Oh, my, badness!*

"Two-point-two million dollars." she repeated in a daze.

"After signing the paperwork, you'll want to check out your new property ASAP," the lawyer advised.

Lacey nodded, speechless.

"Your great-uncle only made one stipulation."

Lacey's fingers tightened on the deed. She knew this was too good to be true.

The lawyer leaned forward, dead serious. "The black cat has access to the premises or you lose ownership."

"Is that all? I love cats. All animals. Just as long as *I* don't have to stay there. I'm really not a 'Boots and Spurs' kind of gal."

* * *

The lawyer leaned back in her massive leather chair after the client left, sighing over the lucky struck-it-rich heir she'd researched. Twenty-five. Too attractive to be single, but her fiancé since high school had died in a car wreck two weeks before their wedding. A teacher. Good with children. Maybe not so good with men or boots and spurs, but girls usually fall in love with horses in their pre-teens, so maybe Uncle Heck's bequest would turn up a match made in Heaven for her.

Unless Uncle Heck had gone to Hell.

* * *

Lacey stood in the warm Reno sunshine, a wheeled travel bag the size of a Great Dane at heel beside her. The Internet warned that Nevada was warm in October but could be cold at night. Her destination was fifteen miles southeast.

The airport cabby couldn't drive that far and had dropped her off at someplace called "Gangsters," a showroom for funky stretch limos lined up in custom colors from Elvis hot-pink to Mafia-funeral black.

A marooned female attracted a pack of salesmen in expensive ice-cream-colored Italian designer suits. Lacey nicknamed her students on the first day of school as a memory device. She'd tag the three now surrounding her as Tall, Dark and Handsome, each interchangeable. "Surrounding" was right. She was five-foot-two, eyes of green.

"This is a casino?" She eyed the neon sign.

"Gangsters' Hotel-Casino is on the Vegas Strip, dear lady," said Handsome.

"We are at Gangsters, Reno," said Tall, "A Nevada-wide custom limo service."

"I don't need a custom limo, but I need to get here." She produced the typed card.

BOOTS AND SPURS, COYOTE WELLS, NEVADA

Black eyebrows lifted in unison. "We know it well," said Dark, "but it's closed. Owner died."

"Well, I'm not dead and I still need to get there," Lacey said.

Tall, Dark and Handsome exchanged the looks that meant she not only didn't know *where* she was going, she didn't know *what* she was getting into.

Tall stepped out of the obviously family cluster. "Gangsters is owned by the Fontana Family brothers, of which we are three of ten. We did business with old Heck, er, Hezekiah Smith, Miss—?"

There were more *T,D and H's?* "Uh, I'm Miss McIver. His great-niece. I inherited the place."

Another round of annoyingly significant glances.

"We'd drive you there gratis, Miss McIver, in honor of your great-uncle Heck," said Tall, "but it's remote and lonely. We'd want you to meet some local residents before we left you there without transportation."

"Very thoughtful," she said, as Dark and Handsome extracted their cell phones. "May I see the limo my uncle hired?"

More glances.

"Certainly," said Tall, "we haven't re-customized it yet." He escorted her inside the showroom of long limos of many colors, but led her to a licorice-shiny black one, and opened a door. The in-the-round interior could have had held a hot tub. Lacey sank onto a cushy black leather seat just inside. Gold fittings shaped as stirrups, riding crops, boots and wheeled spurs shone like 24-carat stars.

Maybe all the gold symbolized Uncle Heck's income source.

She looked up. "The ceiling is upholstered in black leather too." She shivered. "I'm sorry, Tall, but it feels like… a really posh hearse. My uncle commissioned *this* for customers out for a good time?"

Tall blinked at her nickname as Dark lowered his head inside the interior almost as black as his hair. "Many signature Vegas businesses maintain theme limos at Gangsters Reno to ferry customers to and from farther locations, Miss McIver."

Behind him, Handsome bowed and smiled. "Don't fret, Miss. Gangsters has found you site-appropriate transportation to Coyote Wells. We contacted your uncle's, er, associate, with news of your arrival."

"Wonderful!" Lacey gladly let Tall, Dark, and Handsome pull her from the low, wallowing seat. They all wore the same heady, leather-scented men's cologne, so she was feeling a bit "transported" already.

"This ride's a bit rough, but ready for the high desert." Handsome stepped aside to reveal another Tall, Dark and Handsome, but definitely not family, standing behind him.

Her eyes still adjusting from the limo's dark interior, Lacey blinked at six-foot-two of Central Casting cowboy-safari guide wearing a many-pocketed khaki jacket and black cowboy hat, pinned up on one side, Aussie adventurer style.

"This," Tall said, proud of producing a solution to her transportation quandary, "is a local rancher. He'll drive you to Coyote Wells. And back again, if you want. Meet Micah Howell."

White teeth flashed in a tanned face sporting the dark, semi-shaven look, making him many rough-road miles away from the city-sleek Fontana brothers. Lacey felt a now-foreign jolt to her stomach that surfed a wave of excitement all the way south of the border she'd lived behind for years.

"Mike," the guy corrected with another dazzling grin, extending a big tanned paw of a hand.

Oh, what white teeth you have, Grandma.

Lacey wondered what twist of fate had conjured this looming specimen of manly impact for one lone Little Red Riding Hood.

"Just have my Jeep, not a limo-smooth ride," Mike said, his thumb alone brushing her whole sensitive palm as his handshake withdrew. Another big-wave ride for Lacey's subdued libido. In the desert!

Mike had made an aw-shucks comment, but his once-over glance at her was swift and thorough. Lacey cringed inside at her flat-heeled travel Sketcher shoes, her bare pale legs and bland, navy, divided skirt and short jacket. She looked down at Mike's footwear. Yup. Cowboy boots, and even slightly scuffed... to boot. No spurs. Yet.

"So you're a neighbor," she said.

He nodded.

"What brings you into Reno?"

He grinned. "A little horseplay."

Was the man boasting of his Second Sin City sex life with a stranger? Lacey reined in her suddenly quivering curiosity and settled on a politely interested expression.

Tall, Dark and Handsome were laughing. Tall slapped Micah—Mike—on the khaki shoulder. "This guy's too modest. He came here to consult on the Grand's Sierra Hotel-Casino's big new horse act."

"Consult?" Lacey asked Mike. "Are you a vet?"

"Only of the military, ma'am."

"Mike's a horse whisperer," Dark explained. "Can just touch them and get what's wrong and fix it."

"That's a... a tremendous gift," Lacey, said, meaning it.

"Sometimes it can feel like a curse." Mike was serious too.

Lacey nodded. It would be awesome to tune into the spirit of living things. Sad, also, if they were ill or hurt. She stared into his eyes, wells of deep blue water, cool and silky in the shade of his hat brim. She mentally shook off another cresting wave of current that swamped her.

"Born with it," Mike said, his gaze still pinning her. "Can't help it." He shrugged.

"Where's your ride parked, Mike?" asked Handsome, breaking the spell by lifting both of Lacey's bags with his own shrug.

* * *

While the Fontana Boys shoved Lacey's bags into the Jeep's rear cargo space, Lacey was confronting the shiny khaki side of what looked like a Hummer meant for Indiana Jones coated with Buttery Beige nail polish. The passenger door announced, "Wrangler Sierra" as in "High Sierra", and the running board step-up hit her leg like a mini-skirt, six inches above the knee.

She struggled to get one foot up, like on a horse, but was instantly cradled, lifted and deposited in a seated position on a buttery-beige leather front passenger seat, so high it almost gave her acrophobia.

While she fought to adjust her divided skirt, Mike slammed the door shut and went around to bound into the driver's seat. He tossed his hat on the dashboard and combed a hand through his thick black hair springing free. "Not a limo," he said, "but the view is impressive."

Lacey needed to break the tension, her tension. "Speaking of views, lucky I was wearing gaucho pants."

"Lucky, depending on your point of view." Mike winked. He donned sunglasses while still watching her.

Lacey hadn't blushed since high school, but her comment *had* been primly school teacher-ish. She'd hung with pre-teens too long. She just felt so "new girl in town." Why had she buried her sunglasses in the carry-on? Mike's expression was concealed while she was bared-faced.

Symphonic music filled the hard-top car. She jerked in alarm.

"It's a longish, bumpy drive," he told her.

"People by the limo-full went back and forth that long to get there? The property must be pretty exclusive to be so profitable."

"Ah, yeah." He smiled. "Nothing like it in these parts. You know the clientele it served?"

"City slickers like me, I imagine. Am I right I could have visited as a guest?"

"Oh, yeah, you could have. I'm not sure you would have."

"I may not know much about horses and Western stuff, but I *am* a quick learner. You have to be when wrangling thirty-five seventh-graders. But what about you? Were you chief 'whisperer' for the Boots and Spurs horses? I'd love to watch you work."

What she watched now was the dark red color suffusing the back of Mike's neck. Was he… shy?

"What kind of operation do you think B&S is?" he asked.

"I just saw the deed. Acres and mineral rights and outbuildings. I assumed it's a dude ranch."

"'Dude ranch,'" he repeated, his deep voice strangled to an even lower level. "Yes, that would be a very good description, but your

Uncle Heck didn't do things quite like everybody else."

"Must have been a lonely life way out here, being an old bachelor prospector. I'm sure the horses were a comfort."

Mike nodded, dead sober, eyes dead ahead. "Yup. Human and horse are one of nature's enduring match-ups."

While Mike drove, Lacey struggled not to study his profile and concentrate on the flat desert landscape stretching forever, unpopulated apparently, as the soaring music filled the vehicle. She sought to say something not stupid. Finally.

"Mike, I'm so excited to know I own horses. I'm a novice. Will you continue on at the dude ranch as head, er, wrangler and whisperer? I can afford the financial arrangements."

"Sure. If you stay."

"For now, at least. Frankly, I was ready for a big change in my life."

"And you have no... entanglements?"

"I'm boarding my dog, Chieftain, until I know the lay of the land. It's pretty wild out here, I know. "

"'The lay of the land,'" Mike repeated in a mutter, sounding as if he was smothering a laugh again.

He made her swoon and *she* made him laugh. What a no-starter!

She tried again. "But Chieftain's a wolfhound, so the jackrabbits had better have good holes."

"*You?* You own a wolfhound?"

"I may look like a city slicker, Mr. Horse Whisperer, but I've always loved and gotten along with animals and I am not some naive young thing."

"Sorry. Still, take a look at the place before you start making plans to send for your dog." Mike nodded to the windshield. He meant "take a look" literally.

Lacey did, and gasped.

A two-story stone Victorian house rose up from the desert flatlands like a mirage. Next to it a small pond was embraced by a huge branched tree, bowing down to it like a weeping willow.

"Ancient hot spring," Mike explained. "The tree's a salt cedar. Big attraction. Separate cottages surround the big house."

"Big house? It's a mansion, Mike! A mansion in the middle of a giant sandbox. No wonder people wanted to come out here. I could move in tonight? Is a bedroom ready?"

"I'm sure one can be found in good order. Martha Applegate stayed on after your great-Uncle died. She'd been housekeeper here for years, and had no place else to go."

"*You* don't need a housekeeper?"

Mike shook his head, laughing. "I just have a small cabin. I work away so often on the surrounding ranches and in Vegas."

Lacey looked over the land along the deserted road, all fenced with barbed wire. "The dude ranch really gave its customers the full-meal-deal of the Old West, sand and sagebrush."

By then Mike had swung the steering wheel hard left onto an asphalt road, leading straight to the house's double wood doors. He stopped, retrieved her bags, and toted them up the three main steps. He used the big brass knocker in the shape of a horseshoe.

"Mrs. Appleby will come quick to show you the, uh, layout. I've got horses to feed."

"Wait," Lacey called after him, turning. Mike was already looking out the Jeep's driver's window, waving a farewell hand.

Lacey turned as the door hinges creaked open and she felt a draft of cool air trapped by the big stone house—and heard an air conditioner hum. Cool.

She walked past the open door into a soaring entry hall with a grand wooden staircase leading to the second story.

"I didn't expect a manor house," she said, taking it all in. "I'm the new owner, Lacey McIver, Mrs. Applegate."

"*Mrs.?*" a woman's mocking contralto answered from behind her. "Never married, not me. Call me Martha."

Lacey turned and almost jumped out of her skin to face a tall, siren-figured woman in her forties who wore black clinging leggings with thigh-high leather boots and a cold-shoulder top, and favored blood-red lips and fingernails. Morticia Addams West.

"Oh. Sorry. I took you for the housekeeper."

Martha tossed her long black hair and waved an elegantly ringed hand. "This is the *house*, and *I* keep it guest-ready. I'll welcome full rooms again soon. An elevator's under the stairs, so we can pick your room. I do microwave-freezer cuisine—and cans for the cat—but the cook will return now we're live and open for business again."

"The cat? That's the cat that 'must remain'?"

"*He* seems to think so," Martha said, looking down.

A large black cat was circling Lacey's luggage with nose rubs and purrs and random black hairs.

"Midnight Louie, Heck called him," Martha said. "He hitches rides in sometimes with Gangsters, but never stays long."

Martha pulled the extended handle of Lacey's large bag behind her like a dog on a leash, her... yup, four-inch bootheels clicking over the slate floor like a snapping whip. The vintage glass and wrought-iron cage elevator opened in the upstairs hall. Lacey stared at rows of doors on either side, each a different style, like Gangsters' limos.

"All the rooms have lavish baths. I suggest for you... "—Martha's tarantula-leg-thick false eyelashes batted when she surveyed Lacey as swiftly as Mike had—"the Victorian Suite."

Abandoning the luggage, Martha strode past the doors, pushing each open with a commanding wave.

"First, your Queen Vicky bedroom. She did what it took to have nine children, after all. Then come the Sultan Suite, the Cossack Suite, the Sheik Suite, the Castle and Crypt suite, the Lugosi Suite, the Leopard Suite, the Captain Jack Suite, the Errol Flynn Suite." Martha rolled her eyes. "That's extra busy. You can add some suites of your own."

Lacey trotted after Martha to peer into large rooms only housing huge beds lavishly draped, with mirrors everywhere.

"I wonder if Gangsters could mirror a limo ceiling," Lacey muttered.

"Gangsters can do anything automotive, dearie. You may find your decor imagination soaring here. We could use some new blood."

"So folks get to have a fancy sleep here after a long, hard day on the trail with the horses," she commented.

Martha stopped dead. "Sleep? Oh, my dear, sleeping is so not the purpose of these bedrooms. We are, after all, in Nevada, home to—"

"Stop!" Lacey slapped the heel of her hand to her forehead. "I forgot that about Nevada. So Uncle Heck ran a legal brothel? I just assumed it was a dude ranch, the outbuildings—"

"'Cupid's Private Love Nests'."

"The outdoor hot spring spa?"

"The 'Love Float'. This is not just any ordinary brothel. 'Ladies' Choice Ranch' is a unique and secret place. Our only clients are women."

"So there are… were… "dudes" in residence. "Now that the ranch is closed, what happened to the, uh, unemployed workers?"

"Oh, scattered here and there," Martha said with a casual hand wave. We can get them back." She eyed Lacey's figure. "You're small but stacked. Once we outfit you in fishnet hose, kinky boots and corsets, you'll have your pick for riding the range every night. And that rosy blush of yours is so damn inciting to our guys, especially some. I was all blushed out thirty years ago. Thank God for rouge and women's liberation."

"Uh, very liberated, I'm sure," Lacey said, remembering how her "not naive" chatter about a "dude ranch" must have had Mike in stitches, the stinker. He could have warned her.

* * *

Martha served microwaved lasagna dinner in the huge chef's kitchen. Midnight Louie dined on Nine Lives canned food on the slate floor. He followed Lacey up to her Victorian bedroom afterwards. The bedrooms' big-screen TVs weren't programmed to inspire sleep, but naked high-jinks that made Lacey blush to herself. *Oh, my goodness! Oh, my badness!*

Lacey pulled out her hotel kit and sleep T-shirt and regarded the high-pillowed four-poster bed with its heavy red velvet drapes. A claustrophobe's nightmare. When she laid her clothes out on what looked like a crimson velvet rocking horse, she turned to find Midnight Louie had made her Tee into a crumpled nest he was lounging on and pummeling with his front paws.

Lacey sighed and slipped nude into the bed. Instead of a top sheet there was a three-inch, featherweight, European eiderdown quilt. She felt like Venus sinking down into her clam shell, not rising. Tomorrow she would call Gangsters, get back to Reno, and sell the place. There must a ton of debased would-be flesh-peddlers in town.

* * *

The next thing she knew, she awoke to a coyote howl in the distance, then a chorus of yips. Of course noisy nights at Ladies' Choice must be the rule. Still, the cries gave her goose bumps. She turned in the bed and felt it sink beside her as she was enveloped in a warm, slightly furry presence.

"No, Louie! No 'Midnight' visitations. I don't sleep with animals."

Uh-oh. Not a cat. A sense of hot, canine panting tickled her left shoulder. A low growl vibrated in her left ear. What lay next to her was six feet-something of naked, warm, slightly hairy man or beast. Caressing fingers on her forehead and jaw were easing fear and tension. His mouth brought warmth and wet to her ear, her mouth. His palms brushed her stiffened nipples and she heard a gruff growl in his throat acknowledging her body's permission.

Not *hers!* This was a dream incited by the blue movie and her dream lover was Mike, and he felt so right as their legs twined and her hips rose and fell to meet his surging body. No, not just Mike. Micah. A singular name for a singular man who'd touched something buried inside her, something walled off and secret, and now all her secrets would be free and the new secrets would be theirs and theirs alone. Subconscious wish fulfillment. Best dream ever.

"Micah," she whispered against his roughened cheek as his head moved down her body. "Yes, you. Yes, yes, yes. Always yes."

And then thought abandoned her and she was lost in a vortex of heat and flesh and seeking, a storm of motion and emotion.

Until... Lacey glimpsed the black cat on the hope chest and panicked.

"I'm awake. Micah. You're real. Not a dream. I don't understand. I'm in love with a figment of my imagination. I don't want you ever to leave, and I never want to wake up."

He tenderly clasped her to him, calmed the storm, brushed the hair back from her face with kisses.

"I *am* real. You don't have to leave, waking or sleeping, we are locked together. Little darling, the moment I met you, I diagnosed a stress fracture of the heart. I saw the flower of your first love and unfolding as a woman that was snatched away from you, body and soul. I can't *not* help a hurting thing. I had to come to you."

"You pity me? I don't need brothel therapy."

"Is that it?" He laughed. "The gift and curse of my 'body and soul whispering' makes me a shape shifter, not a werewolf, but dominant on the canine side. Not always, but always human at heart. I never was available as a resident 'dude'. Heck kept a couple horses for him and Martha. I tended them."

"'Not always canine'. So you were the black panther I saw on the

63

hope chest?

"Just making sure you were safe and sane after discovering Ladies' Choice Ranch and its purpose. All the men here were multi-talented, you might say. Creatures of the night. The desert hot spring is a mystic font for those who were thought cursed with paranormal personas, *gifts* Martha convinced them. She's the dorm mother for the exiled, the legends, the angst-ridden vampires and werewolves and lingering ghosts who never fit in and never died. Here they're made almost human, special, loved and wanted, and able to love and give it without peril."

"Stop! I'll have to rethink everything. I'm so confused. Except that I love and want you madly, Micah Howell, despite any wolfish ways. Or maybe because of them. It doesn't matter. You've healed wounds I didn't know I had."

"Wolves mate for life, you know."

"No, I didn't know. I'm glad you mentioned it."

Lacey sat up in bed, dislodging him momentarily. "Micah?" She said the name with such love that he buried his face between her neck and shoulder, circling her throat with love nips.

She would not allow him to distract her for this once.

"Micah Howell," she said dreamily, snarkily too, then slapped his shoulder. "Micah. Wait a minute."

He looked up, puzzled, into her eyes.

"*Howell*. Howl. I totally missed that clue. You'll be making that up to me for a good long time, Mr. Big Bad Wolf. After all, one bad good deed deserves another."

"Oh, and another, and, oh my, yes, another."

It was then the big black cat stalked out of the Victorian Suite, tail held high. He would come and go, Martha said, but unlike Lacey, he was not bound to be here forever happily ever after.

"About Chieftain… he's not—" Lacey murmured into Micah's ear.

"You didn't *fix* him!" Micah sounded horrified.

"He's still a pup. No. Not yet."

Micah laughed. "I imagine he'll become the king of the coyotes around here. First crack at all the pretty little bitches."

"Language!"

"No worries, teach. Totally breed appropriate. I'll have a little talk with him."

"A whispered talk?"

"*Uh-huh.* There's a little wolf in every dog. But no bedroom privileges for him."

"What about when Midnight Louie visits?"

"Cats, fine. He brings out the panther in me and you are gonna love that."

5

IGASHO THE IMMORTAL

Kathy Love

"I cannot believe we are actually doing this," Lindsay said, looking around at the milling crowd with a critical squint. Well, her squint was only partially critical. The other part was due to the glaring sun and the dust. She didn't know if she'd ever get used to how dry it was here.

"We are in Nevada. We have to go to at least one rodeo," Mia said, as if that was an actual law written down somewhere.

Lindsay made an unconvinced face, as she sidestepped a kid running toward them, waving a turkey leg as big as his arm. The boy was followed by a band of equally rambunctious kids, several of them dressed for the occasion in cowboy hats and boots.

In the distance amid the flashing lights and carnival rides and concessions, Lindsay heard a band covering an old Waylon Jennings song that she could remember her grandfather playing on his ancient record player when she'd visited him and Grammy in the summers as a kid. Staying with her grandparents in rural West Virginia was as close to "country" as she'd ever been.

"I'm from Manhattan," Lindsay pointed out. "I'm not sure this is my scene."

"And I'm from Vermont," Mia said. "What do I know about rodeos? But I'm here, so I'm going to check it out."

Lindsay sighed. She supposed her housemate was right. They were here doing an internship at Desert Valley Hospital from their university in New York, which had seemed a bit like losing the lottery. Not that Desert Valley Hospital wasn't a great facility. It was. Top of its field in blood disorders, which was both Lindsay and Mia's medical concentration.

But it was in the middle of nowhere. And so damned sunny. She raised a hand to shield her eyes. As she did, her heel caught the loose gravel of the midway. She pitched forward, making a small noise as she tried to catch herself.

Suddenly, a shadow fell over her, and a pair of strong hands curled around her upper arms, just moments before she would have face-planted into the dusty dirt. She squinted up at her rescuer, her eyes taking a moment to focus with the change of light. But when they did, she thought she must be seeing things.

She was looking up at a very tall man, lean and muscular, with long waves of dark hair topped with a top hat, intense dark eyes and white makeup all over his face. White makeup with red paint, defining his full lips, and black makeup coming to points and swirls around his eyes.

She blinked. She had to be seeing things.

When she opened her eyes again, she was greeted by the same made up face and penetrating eyes.

"Are you okay?" the man asked, his voice decidedly more normal than his attire. In fact, it was quite nice. Deep with a slight drawl.

"I'm—I'm fine."

He studied her a moment longer, then nodded. "Have fun. And be careful."

With that, he turned and continued down the midway. As he strolled away, Lindsay noticed his muscular frame was covered in a dusty, red topcoat with tails, black pants and worn boots. And gloves. He looked like a goth ringmaster from some bizarre circus.

"Wow," Mia said, gaping after the man and Lindsay wasn't sure if she was confused or impressed.

"Well, you don't see that every day," Lindsay finally said.

Mia laughed. "And you thought this would be boring."

No, this definitely was not boring, Lindsay decided as she followed her friend into the throng of rodeo revelers.

* * *

67

Once Lindsay was settled down in the stands with nachos and a cold beer, she had to admit she wasn't miserable. In fact, the energy in the arena was kind of contagious. A group of girls, who appeared to be in their late teens, hung over the railings, trying to catch a glimpse of someone, probably one of the riders. Other spectators held up hand-painted signs. She saw several different names, but the majority of the signs said one name in particular: Igasho the Immortal.

"Who do you think Igasho the Immortal is?" Lindsay murmured to Mia.

Mia shrugged. "Maybe a rider. Or maybe a horse. That's a pretty unusual name."

Lindsay nodded and took a drink of her beer. Then she noticed the woman in front of them glancing over her shoulder in their direction, a small, knowing smile on her lips. She probably realized she and Mia were rodeo virgins. Lindsay took another sip of her beer.

A voice crackled to life over the loudspeakers, proclaiming the events were about to begin. The stadium responded with a roar of cheers. Lindsay looked around. Well, there was no denying the locals were really into this.

The disembodied voice returned to enthusiastically announce that barrel racing would be the first event. Lindsay didn't know what barrel racing was, but she quickly figured out that it required the riders, who were all women, to race their horses around barrels as fast as they could without touching them. Lindsay had to admit the event was entertaining and quite thrilling. Still, she found her gaze leaving the action to look around the stands, although she wasn't exactly sure what she was hoping to see.

Then she spotted him, and she realized he was exactly who she was looking for. The tall man with the tailcoat and top hat. He wasn't seated in the stands with the other spectators. He leaned on the railings surrounding the arena, watching the event. Then his head turned, his gaze scanning the crowd as if he could sense she was watching him. His gaze stopped and seemed to focus directly on her. Even from a distance, she could see the intensity of his dark eyes.

Just when she was certain he was looking at her, he returned his attention back to the riders. Lindsay shook her head at her own silliness. As if he could even see her amidst all the other onlookers. She took a drink of her beer and watched the action again, although her gaze did return to the man several times. He really was rather fascinating.

The barrel racing ended, and the next event was bronco riding.

"They have to be crazy," Mia said, while she watched the first rider holding onto the wildly bucking bronco for dear life.

"Definitely," Lindsay agreed, but as her eyes returned to where the tall, made-up man was for the umpteenth time, she wondered if she was the crazy one. Why was she suddenly so intrigued by the strange man? Because he was oddly attractive, even in his clownish makeup and bizarre clothes.

"Oh no," Mia gasped and Lindsay looked away from the man to see another rider, flat on his back, thrown by the highly irritated horse. The rider rolled aside just as the horse's front hooves would have slammed down on him.

"That has got to hurt," Mia stated and popped a tortilla chip her mouth. Lindsay smiled at her friend's rapt expression. Clearly Mia was becoming a rodeo fan.

Maybe Lindsay was too. She glanced back to where the odd mystery man had been, but now the spot was empty. She looked for the conspicuous top hat but saw no sign of him.

A wave of disappointment washed over her, and again, she wondered about her own sanity. Why did she feel so upset to see the odd man was gone?

The announcer's voice blared over the speakers in a rousing tone, declaring the next event would be bull riding.

"Great, more guys flung to the ground by pissed off animals," Mia said wryly, then she took a deep drink of her beer as if to brace herself. But the anticipation in her eyes seemed to contradict her words.

Lindsay chuckled to herself. "You're going to make me come to another one of these, aren't you?"

Mia readily nodded. "Hells yeah."

Lindsay laughed again, but the sound died on her lips. There he was. Her painted, mystery man. But this time, he wasn't behind the railings. He was inside them.

She watched in amazement as he stayed on the field as the first rider and bull were released from the gated box. The bull bucked and kicked across the gouged dirt of the arena until the rider was finally thrown. Then to Lindsay's dismay, the mystery man ran toward the angry animal, waving his arms to distract the huge beast away from the fallen rider.

The bull immediately turned his wrathful attention on him. Lindsay gasped as the giant, enraged animal charged at him. But the man darted with unusual speed out of the bull's way. He did it again and again. Getting the bull's attention, then racing and dodging out of the way, just before the animal could gore him with his long horns.

"Hey, isn't that the guy who caught you before you fell?"

Lindsay nodded at Mia's question, but gave no further response. She was too mesmerized, and appalled, to take her eyes off him for even a moment.

She moved forward on her seat, and the mystery man did this again and again with each rider and each furious bull. Twice, the bulls managed to catch up with him, lifting him fully into the air with a fierce jerk of their head and horns. Both times, the man flew through the air only to land on his feet like a circus acrobat. Or a superhero. He even gave an exaggerated bow to the audience after each attack, waving his top hat with the flourish of an elegant gentleman.

Lindsay was only vaguely aware of the crowd cheering wildly for the extremely athletic and utterly crazy man. She was too amazed at what she was seeing.

Finally, the bull riding event was done, and the man gave another dramatic bow. The audience went mad, screaming and applauding. He straightened, and for a moment, Lindsay had the feeling again he was looking right at her. Then he loped across the arena and jumped over the railings with the agility of a cat.

Lindsay sat back in her seat, feeling strangely bemused. "He's a rodeo clown."

The woman in front of them, who had given them an amused look earlier, turned to look at them again.

"That's Igasho the Immortal."

* * *

"Okay," Mia said, taking a seat at one of the crowded picnic tables where Lindsay had managed to save two seats. She set a paper plate loaded with two corndogs and a pile of fresh-cut fries between them. "You have to admit that was some of the craziest crap you have ever seen?"

"Oh, I can't deny that," Lindsay agreed readily.

"And you were rescued by the star of the whole show." Mia widened her eyes with amused amazement.

Lindsay laughed, but just thinking about where Igasho the Immortal's hands had touched her, made her skin tingle. She took a sip of her beer, telling herself the heat and sun and craziness of what she'd just watched was affecting her head.

Mia took a bite of one of the corn dogs, munching thoughtfully. "It's weird, but that rodeo clown guy–he's kinda sexy."

Lindsay didn't say anything, reaching for a fry instead. But Mia was right. He was kinda sexy. And she couldn't seem to get him out of her head.

"So, what should we do after this?" Mia asked.

Lindsay pretended to consider her friend's question, then said casually, "I like the band that's playing right now. Maybe we should head over there and check them out."

Mia smiled, clearly not buying Lindsay's offhanded tone. "Hmm, I didn't know you were a country music fan."

Lindsay shrugged. "I can take it or leave it."

"And maybe your hero Igasho the Immortal will be there too."

Lindsay made a face at her friend. Sometimes her friend was way too perceptive.

* * *

The band was good, playing a fun mixture of popular country and classic rock hits. And to both Lindsay and Mia's surprise, they ran into a few people they knew from the hospital. But Lindsay only half-followed their conversation. Lindsay's attention kept turning to the crowd, searching for any signs of a top hat and white greasepaint. To her disappointment, she hadn't spotted either.

"Do you want drink?" Lindsay leaned in to ask Mia, who was chatting with one of the male nurses from the hospital.

Mia shook her head. "I'm good right now."

"I think I'm going to go get a water."

Mia nodded, already back in conversation with their coworker.

Lindsay wandered through the crowd, heading toward the concession stand that advertised pretzels, deep-fried Twinkies, soda and cold beer. She stopped at the end of a short line, fishing in her jeans pocket for her money.

"No more tripping while I was gone?" a voice said, close to her

71

ear.

Lindsay started, even though she instantly recognized the voice. She turned, looking up at the man next to her.

Igasho stood beside her, towering over her. He still wore the greasepaint on his face, but he no longer wore the tailcoat or top hat. Now he had on a loose, button-down, black shirt and faded jeans. The face paint stood out even more against his everyday clothing. Yet, he was still striking. Especially his eyes. They were almost hypnotic.

"Umm, so far, so good." Lindsay stammered, suddenly feeling like a teenager being approached by the coolest boy in school. Which in a weird way was pretty accurate. He had been the star of the rodeo. Even now, as she looked past him, she saw others, especially women shooting admiring looks in Igasho's direction.

"Can I buy you a beer?" He smiled, and she no longer noticed the other people watching him. His smile was gorgeous. His lips were wide and full, but not so full they looked feminine, and his teeth were white and straight.

"O–okay."

"So how did you like the rodeo?" he asked, not seeming to notice her nervousness.

"I–I liked it. You were very impressive."

He bobbed his head slightly, his expression humble. "Thank you. It's a fun side gig."

"This isn't your full-time job?"

He shook his head, and she liked the way his long waves framed his face.

"No, I'd have to travel the rodeo circuit to work full-time, and I've done enough traveling in my lifetime. I only do this rodeo. It's fun, but not too much of a commitment."

She started to ask him what he did do for a living, but an impatient employee at the order window barked out, "What can I get you?" But as soon as she saw who she was waiting on, her sour expression turned to a sweet smile–for Igasho anyway.

Beers in hand, Igasho gestured with his head toward the midway. "Would you like to take a walk around?"

Lindsay thought about Mia, but decided her friend seemed just fine with their coworkers. "Sure."

"My name is Igasho," he offered as they strolled down the

midway, which made Lindsay laugh. He cast her a sidelong look, his drawn-on eyebrow raising wryly.

"Sorry," she said immediately, realizing he might think she was laughing at his unusual name. "It's just that your name would have been hard to miss. All the signs. All the people shouting it."

He nodded, still managing to look humble. "Oh, right. Rodeo fans can be pretty hardcore."

"I saw that. And I'm Lindsay."

"Hi, Lindsay."

Her heart swooped in her chest at the cute way he said her name. Holy crap, she couldn't remember a guy ever making her feel this way. Giddy and nervous and definitely attracted. And he wore clown makeup.

"So what do you do, Lindsay?"

And there was that unusual drawl, slow and sexy. She loved how her name sounded when he said it.

"I'm actually finishing up my degree in medicine. I'm here doing an internship at Desert Valley hospital."

He looked impressed. "So, you are gorgeous and intelligent."

The compliment would have been dripping cheese from any other man. But from Igasho, it sounded sincere and sweet.

"Well, I'm not sure about that, but thank you."

To her surprise, he caught her hand and pulled her over to the side of the midway, until they were in the shadows behind the back side of the "Pick a Duck" game, standing among all the thick power cords that ran electricity to the surrounding games and food stands.

"I'm sorry," he said, when he saw her startled look. "I just wanted to get away from the crowd." He frowned as if he was struggling to find the right words to continue. "This is going to sound really strange. I certainly don't know you, but as soon as I first saw you today, I had the strangest sensation that I'd met you before."

Lindsay knew his admission should have unnerved her, especially since she was standing in the waning sunlight, away from the crowds, with a stranger. But she didn't feel nervous at all. In fact, she'd never felt safer.

"I'm sure this is especially weird, since I'm standing here with clown makeup on," he added.

Lindsay laughed. "Well, I have to admit that, yes, it is pretty unusual. But I also have to admit, I felt the same way." Had she really just told him that? This was nuts.

He smiled, his painted lips somehow so sexy.

"Do you believe in fate? Or destiny? Or whatever?"

Lindsay wasn't sure she did. Until this moment.

She stared at him, then nodded. "I guess I do."

His gaze roamed her face, then returned to meet hers. His dark eyes burned, so intense, Lindsay couldn't have looked away if she wanted to, but she didn't want to. She wanted to stay lost in his penetrating gaze forever.

Then, as if in slow motion, Igasho's head lowered, his lips coming down to hover just above hers. She could smile his scent, masculine and better than any cologne. She stared at him for a moment, then closed her eyes. She waited, wanting those wide, full lips on hers. And she wasn't disappointed.

His mouth brushed against hers, teasing, testing. Then they captured her, his lips soft and firm at the same time. Without hesitation, her arms came up around his broad, strong shoulders and she kissed him back. He pulled her tight against his body, and she could feel his muscles, his strength, the utter power of him. She moaned and melted into him.

She wasn't sure how long they stood, melded together, their mouths and bodies clinging to each other. His mouth left hers and he kissed his way down her cheek to the tender skin of her jaw and neck.

He pressed open-mouthed kisses against her sensitive flesh, his tongue tasting her. She let her head fall back and his arms hold her weight, unable to do anything but revel in the feeling of him all around her. Her body pulsed with need and hunger, and desire stronger than she could ever remember. She felt a sharp pain at the place where he kissed her, but the pain was instantly transformed into the most intense ecstasy she'd ever experienced. Her knees buckled and she cried out, the sound broken and raw. His hold tightened as he held her, as he pleasured her. She shuddered and her back arched and an orgasm tore through her, so violent, so glorious that she cried out again.

Igasho lifted his head once the last tremor rippled through her body. His eyes burned, bright and glittering. His chest rose and fell as if he was as overcome as she was. He stared down at her, brushing her dark hair away from her face, his touch tender and almost worshipping. Then he kissed her, his lips flavored with a tang of something she didn't recognize.

"Oh, Lindsay," he said, and he lifted his head and studied her. She could hear amazement in his deep voice, but she could also sense a little dismay in those two small words.

She didn't understand any of this. Who was this man? What had he just done to her?

He held her a few seconds longer, then carefully helped her steady her weight back onto her feet.

"I will see you again, my Lindsay," he whispered against her ear, then he released her.

With that, he turned and left her, standing dazed and sated among the shadows and tangled power cords of the midway.

After several moments, she gathered her wits and her physical satisfaction gave way to humiliation. What had she just done? She wasn't even sure. But one thing was certain, she never would have believed she'd be the type of woman to go off into the bowels of a seedy carnival with a stranger and make out with him. Not that that was just making out. Her legs still quivered like jelly from the aftermath of Igasho's mouth on her neck.

She paused at the bright lights of the food carts and games. A barker shouted out for passersby to try their luck.

Yeah, she didn't need to get lucky again.

She straightened her hair and her spine, then stepped back into the throng of people. As she made her way toward the bandstand, she couldn't help feeling that people were looking at her. She tried to ignore the sensation, telling herself it was her own guilt over her behavior making her feel so watched and exposed.

Self-consciously, she touched her lips that still burned from Igasho's kisses. Her fingers came back smudged with red greasepaint. Then she knew it wasn't her imagination. People were looking at her.

She cast a look around, trying to find any reflective surface where she could see herself. Up ahead was a funhouse, its bright lights blinking and beckoning. She rushed in that direction, apologizing to several people she bumped into in her haste.

Then she saw it: one of those mirrors that manipulated reflections to appear tall and thin or short and fat. She headed that way, waiting for a group of laughing kids to finish admiring their distorted images. Finally, they moved to get in line for the funhouse.

Lindsay hurried over to the mirror, pausing at her reflection. Her features twisted in the bowed glass, but she could see the red and white and black makeup smeared around her mouth and across her cheek. As if Igasho had branded her.

Oh, dear God, talk about the ultimate walk of shame.

She gaped around, looking for something to use to wipe the paint off. Seeing nothing, she balled up the hem of her shirt and wiped away the traces of what had happened. Not that she'd ever be able to erase the memory as easily.

Once her face was clean, she still stared at her misshapen features. She didn't recognize herself. What had she just done? She noticed some red still clinging to her neck. She used her hem again to swipe at the lingering traces of Igasho.

But when she inspected her neck and then her shirt, she saw this smear wasn't the greasy bright red of makeup, this was darker red and soaked into her shirt like liquid.

Blood.

She inspected her neck, but the wavy, distorted mirror revealed nothing but a slight redness where his lips had kissed her.

Great. All she needed now was Mia asking why she'd gone to get water and come back with a hickey.

Mia. Her friend had to be wondering where she'd disappeared to for some long. She gave her face and neck one last cursory scrub, then strode back to the bandstand. The band still played, and Lindsay picked her way through the crowd, searching for her friends.

They were right where she'd left them, still talking and dancing.

"Hey," she greeted Mia. "I'm sorry I took so long."

Mia frowned at her. "No problem. You were only gone for a few minutes." Her friend noticed Lindsay's frazzled state. "Are you okay? Where's your water?"

Lindsay shook her head, suddenly feeling very disoriented. She hadn't gotten the water. And she had no idea what happened to the beer that Igasho had bought her. Everything felt so surreal.

"I think I need to go," Lindsay said. The crowd and the music were suddenly too much, closing in on her, making it hard to breathe.

"Sure," Mia said. "It is getting late and you do look kind of pale."

They both said their goodbyes to their coworkers, then made their way to the brown, dried field that served as the parking lot.

Lindsay didn't talk on the ride home, and she was thankful that

Mia seemed to understand she wasn't up to saying much.

Once they were back to the small, stucco house they were renting for their stay here and Lindsay was inside in the cool A/C, she felt a little better.

"Are you sure you're okay?" Mia asked, her brow furrowed with concern.

"Yeah, I think the heat just got to me. And I'm tired from our long hours at the hospital."

Mia seemed to accept her excuse. "I get that. I'm starting nights tomorrow. I'm sure that will knock me out."

Lindsay nodded. "Well, I'm going to head to bed."

"Sleep well."

Lindsay was tempted to tell her that she doubted that would happen, but decided against it. That would lead to having to explain what happened with Igasho. She wasn't ready to share any of that.

"Good night."

Once in her bedroom, she pulled off her smudged and smeared T-shirt, tossing the garment into her laundry bin. Thankfully, Mia hadn't noticed that. Her friend would have definitely put two and two together if she'd seen the white and red and black greasepaint. But it was the blood that disturbed Lindsay that most.

In just her bra and jeans, she went to her bathroom to better inspect her neck. When she turned on the light, she half expected to see the same distorted face in her mirror that she'd seen outside the funhouse. But aside from looking pale and a little mussed, she looked normal. In fact, away from the lights, crowds and sounds of the rodeo, she almost felt like she might have imagined everything that happened there. Maybe she'd imagined everything. All a hallucination brought on my heat and beer.

She turned her head, examining the place where she'd wiped away the droplet of blood. She leaned over the sink to get a closer look. On her neck, an inch or so below her earlobe, she saw two small welts.

She touched them, Two small bites. Had Igasho done that?

She frowned, then straightened away from the mirror. No. That was impossible. They were bug bites or something. She left the bathroom.

She just needed a good night's sleep and to put this weird night behind her.

* * *

Several days passed and Lindsay fell back into her routine of work and studies. She started to believe the night of the rodeo was indeed some strange hallucination.

"I'm off," Mia said, coming through the dining room with her lab coat, purse and car keys in hand. "It's my last night shift for a while. Thank God. My sleep schedule is a mess."

Lindsay looked up from the reports she was studying. "And I get to start them in the next couple weeks."

Mia made a face. "Ah, life in the world of medicine."

Lindsay nodded with a sigh.

"But I hear that a new doctor is starting soon. I also heard through the grapevine that he's an expert in rare blood disorders. *And* he's a total hunk." Mia wiggled her perfectly arched brows. "That could be highly interesting."

"I'm actually going over some of his research right now. Dr. Wilson gave me some of the new doctor's reports to review. It is very interesting."

Mia rolled her eyes. "I was talking about his looks. Not his actual work."

Lindsay laughed and waved to her friend as she disappeared out the door. She returned to reading the incoming doctor's research. His name was Dr. Moon and he'd studied blood, primarily of Native Americans and their descendants. From what he'd discovered, the blood types of Native Americans was more resistant to certain blood disorders, which if they could pinpoint what made them more resistant, could help slow down and perhaps ultimately cure several diseases.

It was fascinating, but it also seemed a little far-fetched. He believed that if certain cells of certain blood types could be isolated, he could potentially cure anything. Lindsay returned to the beginning of the report, trying to understand how this could possibly work, but her reading was interrupted by a knock on the front door.

She looked at her cell phone. It was almost eleven. Who would be here this late? She hesitated, trying to decide if she should just ignore whoever it was. Another knock echoed through the silent house.

Carefully, Lindsay pushed back her chair and tiptoed to the door. She hesitated, then squinted through the peephole.

78

Immediately, she pulled back, stunned at who she saw on the other side of the fisheye lens.

It *couldn't* be him. She peered through again. He no longer wore clown makeup, but from his hair and his build, she could still tell it was Igasho. What was he doing here?

Hand on the doorknob, she debated what to do. It seemed like insanity to let him in. After all, whether they had kissed or not, she barely knew him. But what had happened had been more than a kiss, had it? She hadn't been able to forget him, that was for sure. But she hadn't heard from him since that night. Of course, he had no way to get in touch with her. Yet, he was here now. Which was pretty creepy in and of itself.

She turned the lock and cracked open the door, only enough to peek out at him.

"Hi, Lindsay," he said, and just like the first time he'd said her name, her heart fluttered.

"Igasho. What are you doing here? How did you find out where I live?"

He smiled, his expression sheepish. "I happened to be at the Desert Valley Hospital and I asked about you."

"The hospital?"

"I had to stop by there, and since I knew that's where you worked, I asked about you. One of the nurses told me where you live."

Lindsay frowned. "I'm pretty sure that's illegal."

"I don't think it's illegal, but I know it's unethical," he admitted with another sheepish smile. "My only defense is I was desperate. After what happened between us, I kind of..." he shrugged. "Well, for the lack of a better word, I kind of freaked. And I left before I had the sense to ask how to reach you."

"You did say you'd see me again," Lindsay said.

"Yes. I knew I would. I just should have been a little more proactive."

"Well, asking a coworker is pretty proactive. And maybe a little stalkerish."

"But stalkerish in only the best way."

She laughed. "Do you want to come in?"

He nodded. But once he was in her small home, they both fell silent, both unsure what to say now.

Finally, she gathered her wits enough to ask, "Would you like a drink?"

"Sure."

She headed to the galley kitchen.

"What would you like?" she called over her shoulder while she perused the fridge. "We have beer, some cheap, white wine, orange juice, milk, wat–" Her last word caught in her throat as she turned to see Igasho standing in the kitchen doorway, his tall, muscular frame making the narrow kitchen feel even smaller. He leaned on the doorframe, his arms crossed over his broad chest. She could see his muscles straining against his T-shirt. His jeans rode low on his slim hips.

He watched her with those intense, almost black eyes. A slight smile curved his full lips. And without the greasepaint she could see how golden and perfect his skin was. He ran a hand through his long, black hair and she got to see how utterly beautiful he was. Sculpted features, like some dark, fallen angel.

"I'm not really in the mood for a drink, actually," he said, but the way his gaze roamed over her, he sure looked like a man who was dying of thirst. And she was a cool glass of water.

"What–what are you in the mood for then?" Her heart raced, because she already knew what his answer would be, and she was in the mood for the very same thing.

He pushed away from the doorway, stalking across the short space to her. His large hand curled around the back of her head and his mouth found hers. His kiss was deep and possessive. Instantly, her knees went weak, and as if he felt her trembling, his hands moved to her waist and he lifted her onto the countertop. He moved so his hips were between her legs and braced his hands on the cabinets, caging her in.

He studied her, his expression intense, hungry. "Lindsay, I've thought of nothing but you all week."

For a moment, she wondered if his words were just a line. But as she stared into her eyes, she knew he spoke the truth. She didn't know how, but she knew it.

"I've been thinking of you too."

He groaned, the sound a low growl deep in his throat, and his lips returned to hers. Soon, they were both tugging at each other's clothes, desperate to touch more of each other. His mouth was moving over her body, down to her breasts… lower still. She sank her fingers into the silky waves of his hair, letting her head fall back against the cabinets as he did delicious and naughty things with his tongue. Suddenly, she felt the same pierce of pain on her inner thigh that she'd felt with him before. And just like that first time, it was immediately followed by the extreme, breath-stealing rush of her release. But unlike last time, he didn't stop at that. He rose and angled her hips until he buried himself deep inside her. And then he drove her over the edge again.

When they were finished, they clung to each other, their breaths coming in harsh rasps, filling the small kitchen.

"That was…" Igasho stopped, whether to find the right words or to catch his breath, Lindsay wasn't sure.

"Unbelievable," she finished for him.

"Yes." He lifted his head from where it rested on top of hers and he smiled down at her. She smiled back, shaken by her behavior, but not regretful. Everything about Igasho seemed right.

He scooped her up in his arms as if she weighed no more than a small child. She squealed at the sudden shift.

"What are you doing?"

"I thought we might do this again, but this time in a bed."

"Oh," she said, surprised, but not about to argue. "My room is through the living room. The door on the left."

* * *

After showing her all the amazing things he could also do in a horizontal position, Lindsay collapsed against Igasho's chest, content and sleepy. Only her curiosity about the man kept her from dozing off into a very satisfied, very exhausted sleep.

"So you said, you've traveled a lot? Where?" She lifted her head to look down at him. He looked very satisfied too as he reached up to stroke the hair away from her face.

"All over, really. But mainly in the States."

"Where were you born?"

"Not far from here. I'm full-blooded Shoshone Indian."

"Really? That's amazing, because I'm about to start working with a doctor who has been studying Native Americans and how their blood seems to have a specific trait that could potentially treat many blood disorders."

"Really? That sounds pretty intriguing."

"It is, but to me, it sounds more like science fiction than science."

Igasho seemed to consider that for a moment. "Well, many things that sounded like science fiction have come to pass."

She shrugged. "Yeah, I guess that is true."

"So where are you from?"

"I grew up in New York City. Manhattan."

He gave her a wide-eyed look. "Ah, a *real* city girl. I bet this is all very wild and rustic for you."

She grinned down at him, touched his face. "I'm quickly deciding I'm a fan of wild and rustic."

He chuckled, then stole a kiss. But she pulled away to give him a startled look of her own. "I don't even know your last name."

"Trollop," he teased.

She gave him a brief pout. "You don't know mine either."

"True... or do I? Lindsay Holmes."

Her eyes widened again. "How did you know that?"

"Your friend at the hospital was very helpful."

Lindsay rolled off him but stayed snuggled up against his side. "She really was. So, what is your last name, since you got an unfair advantage?"

"Hmm, I think I'll make you guess. But here's a hint, it is something you probably see nearly every day."

"Well, that narrows it down."

He laughed again.

* * *

The next morning, Lindsay woke to the sound of her alarm clock and an empty bed. She frowned, looking around for any signs of Igasho, only to find a note on the pillow he'd used last night.

She opened it, eager and afraid all at once. She was glad he hadn't just left with no word, but she was afraid it would say something along the lines of "Thanks for the good time. See you around."

But instead, in bold, masculine handwriting, it read,
See you tonight. 7 PM.
–I

She supposed she should be a little off-put by the assumption of the note, but she wasn't. She knew he just wanted to see her again, as much as she wanted to see him. She read the note again, then placed it on her nightstand and rolled out of bed. It would have been nice if he could have stayed the whole night, but she suspected he needed to go home and get ready for work. Not that she knew what he did for work. Or his last name for that matter. Although, not from a lack of guessing.

She wandered into her bathroom and turned on the shower. She looked at herself in the mirror. Her tousled hair and flushed skin revealed a woman well loved.

She pushed back the shower and started to step in, when a blotch of red on her inner thigh caught her eye. It was a tiny patch of dried blood. There were two red welts, just like the ones she'd seen after kissing Igasho the first time. She prodded them, but they didn't hurt.

Weird.

Maybe she needed to consider hiring an exterminator.

* * *

During the next few weeks, if Lindsay wasn't at work, she was with Igasho. And he was proving to be perfect. Smart. Funny. Attentive. Thoughtful. Gorgeous. An amazing lover.

"He really is perfect," Mia said at the breakfast table, after Lindsay shared the details of their previous night's date; dancing lessons at a salsa bar.

"He's even a great dancer," Lindsay told her friend.

Mia groaned. "Where can I find a hot rodeo clown?" She grimaced. "Who even knew there was such a thing as a hot clown, rodeo, or otherwise."

Lindsay made a face, as if to say she certainly never knew such a thing existed. But she did now. She sighed. "The thing is, I'm starting my night shifts tonight, so I don't know how much I'll get to see him over the next couple of weeks."

Mia pondered that as she took a bite of her peanut butter on toast. "That's true. He never does come around during the day, does he?"

Lindsay shook her head. "Even on the weekends, we usually stay up all night and sleep all day. Or just laze around in his apartment, watching movies and ordering takeout."

"Which also sounds pretty perfect," Mia added.

Everything was perfect, and she hoped it would stay that way, even if she couldn't see as much of him.

* * *

When Lindsay got to the hospital that night, she was greeted at the nurses' station by two of her coworkers, Amy and Jessica.

"Dr. Moon is starting tonight. So you'll be doing your rounds with him," Amy informed her.

"Okay," Lindsay said, curious to meet the man.

"He's totally gorgeous," Jessica added.

"Really?" Lindsay said, not particularly interested in that fact. She already had gorgeous, and she doubted this guy could rival Igasho.

"He's in the office next to Dr. Wilson's. He said for you to go there to meet with him before you start your rounds," Amy said.

"Okay."

"Did I mention he's totally hot?" Jessica called after Lindsay as she started to walk away.

Lindsay laughed and shook her head. "Yeah, I think you might have said something along those lines."

Lindsay headed down the corridor. Maybe she was just a little curious as to what this guy looked like.

She knocked on the door and heard a muffled voice from the other side. She opened the door and stepped inside, just as the man in the high-back office chair stood to greet her.

"Hi, Lindsay."

Lindsay blinked, knowing that voice and face as well as her own. "Igasho? What are you doing here?"

He smiled and raised his hands. "I'm Dr. Moon."

Lindsay stared at him for a moment, confused. "Well, I finally know your last name. But why wouldn't you tell me you were going to be working with me?"

"Because I was trying to figure out how to convince you to stay on here after your internship and help me with my research."

Again, she couldn't figure out why he'd kept this such a secret. Being a researcher was exactly what she'd hoped to do with her medical degree. She'd told him as much during one of their late-night talks.

"You know that's what I'd hoped to do with my degree." She

shook her head, not following any of this.

"Well, I know you have some doubts about the work I'm doing." She still didn't follow.

"Plus," he added, "I'm also hoping you'll agree to be more than just my research partner."

She gaped at him. He couldn't be asking what she thought he was asking. "Are you asking me to marry you?"

He nodded, and she noticed the blue velvet box sitting in the center of his desk.

A rush of joy filled her. It was quick, but she knew she loved him. And she knew he loved her.

She opened her mouth to say yes. A thousand times yes, but he raised a hand to stop her.

"Before you make up your mind, I have one more thing to tell you."

He rose and came over to hold her hands. "You've read my research papers. You even mentioned that my findings and my hypostases sound like science fiction. And you were right about that."

Lindsay frowned, not following.

"Linds, I am hundred percent Shoshone. And I was born here. But, I was born over five hundred years ago."

She gaped at him. Here it was, the moment when she discovered he really was too good to be true. He was crazy. Like, certifiably crazy.

"I know how this sounds," he said, clearly seeing the disbelief on her face. "But it is true. My tribe must have had some type of mutation in our blood line. Somehow our cells constantly regenerate. They don't deteriorate as we age. In fact, we hit a certain age, which seems to vary for each of us, and then we remain physically that age."

"That isn't possible."

He shrugged. "It is. I'm proof. And there are others of us too."

No. This was nuts. She tried to pull her hands away.

"But we do require something to keep our cells regenerating."

"And what is that?" She knew her voice sounded a little hysterical, but in this case, she thought that was probably the only acceptable reaction.

"We need blood."

Her eyes widened. "You are not saying what I think you are saying."

He nodded. "I'm a vampire."

"Okay, this is legitimately crazy."

"I'm a vampire, but it's not like in movies. I don't kill people. I don't drain their bodies of blood. I don't sleep in a coffin or turn into a bat. I eat and drink and breathe. I do have to avoid the sun, but I'm not going to burst into flames or anything if I do go out in it. I do everything anyone else does, I just happen to need blood to stay how I am now."

She shook her head. "You do know how crazy this sounds, right?"

"I do."

She stared at him, trying to read his expression. He had to be joking, didn't he? Blood humor or something? But his dark gaze was sincere. And concerned.

"So, have you taken blood from me?"

He looked away, then glanced back at her with one of his sheepish looks that she knew so well, and loved.

"Yes."

She waited for the idea to revolt her, but oddly it didn't. "When?"

"Every night from that very first night at the rodeo."

The shot of pain. The small welts, which she had continued to find on different places on her body.

"I tried to stay away from you. I truly did. But there is something strong between us. I know you feel it too. When I talked about fate, I meant it. I feel like you were somehow brought here to me."

She did too, but she wasn't about to tell him that. Instead, she said, "What? To be your lunch?"

He gave her a pained look. "When I feed, I only need a small amount, and once I get that amount, then complete satisfaction fills us both."

Well, she couldn't deny that one.

"Let me see," she demanded. He looked at her, and then like an obedient child showing his mother that he'd swallowed his medicine, he opened his mouth. To Lindsay's amazement, right in front of her very eyes, his two front teeth elongated into fangs like those of a snake. Without thinking, she reached out and touched them. They sure felt real.

"So you don't kill?"

He shook his head. "It kind of goes against the Hippocratic oath."

"So that's why you can be a rodeo clown? The greasepaint protecting your skin?"

He nodded.

"And that's why you are so fast? And you can take hits from the bulls and remain unhurt?"

"Oh, it hurts. I just recover very quickly."

She tugged her hands away from him, and this time he released her. She wandered across the room, putting space between them so she could think about all he'd told her. After several moments, she turned back to him.

"So you want to essentially use yourself as a resource to help other people with diseases?"

"Yes, I do. And I want you to help me do that."

"And I would be Mrs. Igasho the Immortal?"

His eyes glittered with hope. "I hope you will be."

"But I will grow old and you will stay the same," she said. That idea nearly killed her. And in that moment, she knew she couldn't imagine not being with him forever.

"Well, my darling," he said, walking toward her, his movements like that of a wild cat, "that is another perk from my bites. When I feed from you, you receive some of my cells back into your body."

"Wait, so as long as you feed from me, I stay young and I get to have the most amazing orgasms ever?

He nodded, his smile wide and devastatingly handsome.

"Well, that sure beats the hell out of Botox," she said wryly.

Igasho laughed and kissed her. "I love you."

"And I love you too, Igasho the Immortal."

6

TICKET TO RENO

Virginia Henley

His green eyes searched her heart-shaped face, then slowly he drew her hand to his mouth and he kissed each fingertip. Lily's insides curled at the intimate gesture as a frisson of pleasure spiraled upward into her heart.

"Your beauty dazzles me. I long to kiss you all over, here and here." He made her aware that she was female, and intimately aware that he was all male, dizzyingly male, dangerously male. He overwhelmed her with his powerful presence as he began to lick and taste her from throat to navel, then his mouth devoured her breasts. He took possession of her mouth just as her scream erupted and kissed her until it turned into a sigh.

She turned her head on the pillow and saw the glittering coins he had placed there. Lily London recoiled and sat straight up in bed, fully awake. "Dear God, that's the third night in a row I've had the same dream!" Lily had no idea who he was, couldn't even recall what he looked like, but the beautiful voice remained clear as a bell in her memory.

Lily pushed the dream away and made a cup of coffee. She chose her lavender dress that complimented her red-gold curls. She knew she must look her best today when she made her rounds of the Hollywood Studios.

* * *

"Sorry, Miss London, nothing today."

Lily London's heart sank for the second time that day. It took all her resolve not to let the deep disappointment show on her face. As a young actress, she knew her face was her fortune. *Let A Smile Be Your Umbrella*, the words to the popular song ran through her mind.

"When does the casting for *Cover Girl* start, Jack, I thought it was today?" she asked the Columbia Studio's casting call boy.

"It's been postponed. Rita Hayworth's been chosen as a cultural ambassador by President Roosevelt's administration and she leaves next week for Brazil."

"Oh, how lovely. I don't suppose you know when she'll be back?" Lily asked hopefully.

Jack shook his head. "Picture's been postponed until next year."

"Thanks, Jack." She left Columbia's costume and casting building, turned onto Gower Street and headed toward the rooming house where she lived with half a dozen other budding young actresses who had come to Hollywood to work in the film industry. Earlier in the day, she had been to Paramount Studios and learned they were still doing post production work on *This Gun For Hire*, starring Alan Ladd and Veronica Lake, and wouldn't be casting for any new musicals for a couple of months.

Lily was down to her last few dollars. She didn't have enough money to pay her rent, let alone shop for supper at the nearby Farmer's Market. The only food she had left in her room were apples. *My luck must turn soon. 1941 was such a promising year for me. I got bit parts in three pictures, then was lucky enough to get a dancing role in Yankee Doodle Dandy.*

The movie had wrapped up in early December, and at the cast Christmas party, Lily had won the raffle prize. It was an airline ticket to Reno, Nevada and three nights at the famous Riverside Hotel-Casino. The idea of using it never entered her head. Instead, she intended to sell it and use the money to refurbish her meagre wardrobe. Two days later, the unimaginable happened. The Japanese bombed Pearl Harbor, and the country was at war.

Lily had grown up in San Diego. Her father had disappeared when she was fifteen, and her mother had told everyone he had joined the Navy. By the number of sailors her mother entertained from the nearby naval base, the tale may have seemed plausible to some, but Lily soon learned they were paying customers. The moment she turned eighteen, she packed her bag and took the bus to Hollywood.

* * *

When she got home, she removed her good clothes, put on an old pair of comfortable slacks, and went to the large sitting room that all the girls shared.

"Did you get anything today, Lily?" her friend Nora Jones asked.

She shook her head. "How about you?"

"No, but when I was at MGM I heard they were going to start a war movie in a couple of weeks."

"Warner Bros. is going to do one too," Betty Howard told them. "They're casting for Across The Pacific next week. I hear they've already signed Humphrey Bogart."

"I bet all the studios will be doing war films now," Nora predicted.

Lily sighed. "I'd so much rather get a part in a musical; dancing comes naturally to me."

"Frank's taking me dancing tonight." Nora rolled her eyes. "He promised to buy me dinner at the swank Roosevelt Hotel."

Lily shuddered inwardly at what Nora was willing to do for the price of a dinner. "Did you remind Frank about the ticket to Reno? He seemed interested in buying it."

"Oh, he changed his mind when Carol Lombard was killed in that plane crash flying home from Nevada. It flew straight into Potosi Mountain."

"That was so sad," Lily said softly. *Nobody wants to fly since that happened. I was counting on the money to pay my rent.*

One by one, each girl left with a man who would be paying for her dinner. All they had to do was "sing for their supper."

* * *

Lily went to her room, lit a candle, then picked up an apple and began to take small bites, trying to savor every mouthful. Sudden panic threatened to choke her. None yet knew of the terrible mess she was in. Until now, she had managed to hide behind a facade of serene confidence, her emotions buried deep within, safely concealed from everyone she knew. Lily stared at the candle flame, mesmerized.

She had no idea what she would do to survive without money. Tomorrow was rent day. She knew she couldn't borrow from any of the other girls. Like herself, they lived on what they got paid for bit parts. She opened her purse to count her money. *Three dollars is all I have in the world.*

Lily opened the envelope that held the ticket to Reno, and read the letter guaranteeing three free nights at the Riverside Hotel Casino. She caught her breath. *Do I dare to use it myself? Perhaps I could win some money.* Her thoughts wavered. *No, I've never been out of California. It's just wishful thinking that I could be lucky enough to win money.* Then another thought came into her head. *I was lucky enough to win the Christmas raffle. Fortune favors the bold!* She'd heard that line in a movie. Perhaps it was true, but Lily knew that real life wasn't a movie.

She was afraid to stay and afraid to go. *I'll let Fate decide.* She took a nickel from her change purse. *Heads I'll go; tails I'll stay and face the music.* Lily flipped the nickel and stared down at the head of the buffalo. She took a deep breath and made the decision to commit one hundred percent to the adventure. She pulled her suitcase from under the bed and packed her best clothes. As she folded her things she thought about her recurring dream. She put it all down to seeing scores of love scenes on movie sets, and of course she'd dreamed about money on her pillow because she needed it so badly.

Chapter Two

Lily got off the bus at the Western Airlines Terminal. Her trepidation was hidden by her confident smile as she approached the counter with her ticket. "I'd like to use this today, if I may?"

"Of course, madam, the next flight departs at 11 a.m." The woman at the counter took her ticket and handed back the return portion. "Seat number 17B."

"Thank you so much. Does the plane land far from Reno?"

"We fly into Hubbard Field, three miles from Reno."

Lily smiled her thanks, relieved that the bus fare shouldn't cost more than a dollar.

When she boarded the plane, she found row 17 and saw that seat A was on the aisle and seat B was next to the window. Imitating other passengers, she lifted her suitcase trying to reach the overhead compartment, when suddenly it was taken from her hands.

"Allow me." The tall man behind her lifted up her suitcase, then

91

put his own bag into the overhead compartment and closed it.

"Thank you," Lily murmured and slid into the window seat.

"My pleasure, ma'am."

Lily stiffened. She knew that voice. It was the one from her recurring dream. She stared at the good-looking man with green eyes and dark hair.

He gave her a puzzled glance. "You look familiar. I've seen you somewhere before."

Lily drew in a swift breath. "Perhaps you've seen me on the screen. I'm an actress."

"Aah, most likely." His glance roamed her face. "Let me guess... you're flying to Reno for a divorce."

Lily's eyes flashed her anger. "How dare you, sir!" She looked him up and down. "Let me guess... you're an actor, flying to Reno for a divorce."

"I suppose I deserved that. I didn't mean to offend you, ma'am," he said ruefully. "Can we start again?"

Her anger melted away quickly. The corners of her mouth curved in a smile, as if she'd enjoyed crossing swords with him.

He held out his hand. "I'm Charles Curry, and I'm not an actor."

She shook his hand and it felt like a current of electricity passed between them. "I'm Lily London."

* * *

Your name is as pretty as your face. You look too sweet and innocent to be an actress, Lily London. Charles Curry had had his fill of actresses and the women of Hollywood. They were driven by ambition, and were either interested in his money or what he could do to further their careers.

When the stewardess served them coffee and a croissant he noticed how Lily's eyes shone with appreciation. He was fascinated by the dainty way she ate, taking small bites and savoring each mouthful as if it were ambrosia. *A female who takes pleasure in food may enjoy other sensual delights.* The thought stirred his imagination.

Just as the stewardess removed their empty cups, the plane seemed to lurch and she staggered about trying to regain her balance. Charles saw a look of sheer panic come over Lily's face, and she grabbed his arm in fear. He put his hand over hers. "Don't worry, there's always a bit of turbulence when we go over the mountains.

We'll be just fine."

* * *

The warmth of his hand and his comforting voice had an amazing effect, as a feeling of calm seeped into her. The turbulence finally stopped and Lily laughed nervously. "I'm so sorry. I've never flown before."

He smiled, and to distract her, he took a business card from his wallet and placed it on her tray table.

Lily picked it up and read: Charles Curry

Curry & Wingfield Productions Ltd.

6000 Sunset Blvd.

Hollywood, California.

Her eyes widened. "Do you produce films, Mr. Curry?" She knew producing meant financing.

"Among other things. My partner and I usually back one a year. We're very selective."

"Have you chosen one for 1942?"

"We have one in mind. That's why I'm going to consult with my partner today. We're considering a war film: *Mrs. Miniver*. It's the story of how an English family copes with war. It's a tear-jerker; it touches the heart."

"Is it for MGM? I heard they were going to do a war movie."

"Yes, MGM, but they need the backing. The interiors can be filmed here, but the exteriors will have to be filmed on location in England, and that costs money."

"Does your partner," she glanced at the card, "Mr. Wingfield, live in Reno?"

He laughed. "His father founded Reno. Made millions mining Nevada gold. Now George owns the Bank of Reno, the Bank Club Casino, and the Riverside Hotel."

"Oh, that's where I'm staying," Lily said.

"Great… I'll give you a lift. My car's at the airport."

"I wouldn't dream of imposing, Mr. Curry."

"Please call me Charles, and it's no imposition, I assure you."

Don't be a fool, Lily, accept the ride. You only have two dollars in your purse. She licked dry lips.

"Thank you so much. That's very kind of you."

* * *

When the plane landed, Charles lifted down both bags and proceeded to carry them to the parking area. He unlocked a cream-colored Lincoln and held the passenger door open for Lily.

She smiled her thanks. "If you live in Hollywood, why do you keep your car in Nevada?"

Charles smiled back. "I only have an office in Hollywood. My home is in Carson City."

"Isn't Carson City famous for its ghosts?"

"Yes, indeed. There are many haunted buildings there. Do you believe in ghosts, Lily?"

"Well, I don't disbelieve. Paramount's back lot is said to be haunted. A wall separates it from the Hollywood Forever Cemetery and it has an extremely eerie atmosphere. Many people claim to have seen Rudolph Valentino. Do you believe in ghosts, Charles?"

"Ah, yes. My grandfather, Abraham Curry, haunts the Carson City Mint, which he built."

"How absolutely fascinating."

The car turned onto South Virginia Street and stopped at the Riverside Hotel's entrance. Charles jumped out, opened her door and retrieved her suitcase. "Lily, will you join me for dinner tonight?"

Lily's smile faded. "I'm sorry… Charles… I have a rule. I don't accept dinner invitations from gentlemen. But thank you for the ride. I truly appreciate it." She walked quickly into the hotel without looking back.

Chapter Three

At the hotel desk Lily signed the register and was given a room key. She declined the offer of help with her suitcase and took the elevator to the third floor, thinking it an amazing coincidence that not only was the Riverside at number 17 on Virginia Street, but her room number was 17, the same number as her seat on the plane.

She unlocked the door, and as it swung open she was both surprised and delighted that the room was furnished in the style of the old west. It had an iron bed, a wooden washstand with a jug and bowl, and a colorful rag rug on the floor. She stepped inside, closed the door, and when she turned around she saw that everything had changed… It was a perfectly normal, modern hotel room with

94

broadloom on the floor and blond oak furniture.

Lily put her hand to her head. *What the devil just happened?* She blinked a few times then glanced around the modern room. "It was exactly like a Western movie set, surely my imagination didn't simply conjure it." She walked over to the dresser and looked at herself in the mirror. Suddenly, she became aware of a man's face reflected in the mirror. *It's Charles Curry!*

Lily whirled around and realized that what she had seen was a painting. She walked over to it and read the name displayed beneath the portrait: Abraham Curry. On the wall next to it was a painting of a building identified as the Carson City Mint. She realized immediately that the man was Charles Curry's grandfather. "The resemblance is uncanny!"

Lily felt strange. Suddenly, her decision to fly to Reno threatened to overwhelm her. Perhaps it was because she hadn't eaten much in the last two days. Slowly, she unpacked her suitcase and hung her clothes in the closet. Then she sat down on the bed and contemplated her next step. She had never been in a gambling casino before and she had no idea how to play faro, keno, blackjack or any of the table games. But since she had no money to play these games anyway, it didn't matter. She would change her two dollars into nickels and play the slot machines.

* * *

The casino floor was crowded and noisy. The center of the room was filled with green-felt tables surrounded by gamblers. Lily made her way to the outside perimeter that was lined with slot machines. She looked down into the cup that held her nickel tokens. *I have 40 chances to win. All I need is a little good luck.* She put a single token into a slot and pulled the lever. The fruit symbols whirled around and all three came up different. Lily repeated the action and the result was exactly the same. Still feeling hopeful, she moved to the next machine, put in her token and pulled the lever. As she moved from machine to machine, watching the cherries, oranges and bananas spin around, her hopes melted away. When she was down to her last three tokens, she decided to go for broke. She put all three into the machine, crossed her fingers and pulled the lever.

Lily couldn't believe her eyes when the slot displayed two cherries and a banana. *I've lost again and all my tokens are gone!* Her heart sank and she felt utterly hopeless. With dragging feet, she took the elevator and retreated to her room.

She locked the door securely and went into the bathroom. When she saw the large, deep tub, her spirits lifted slightly. "I'll take a bath. It will be such a luxury not to have to share the bathroom with five other girls."

As Lily lay in the warm water, she refused to dwell on her predicament. She firmly put off until tomorrow all her cares and worries. Her thoughts drifted back over everything that had happened today.

She smiled as a vision of Charles Curry came into her mind. Not only was he good-looking, with a mesmerizing voice that threatened to melt her bones, he was a film producer. *Who knows what tomorrow will bring?*

Lily felt relaxed all over. She curled up in the bed and turned on the radio. As Bing Crosby crooned *Be Careful It's My Heart,* she drifted off to sleep.

* * *

His green eyes searched her heart-shaped face, then slowly he drew her hand to his mouth and he kissed each fingertip. Lily's insides curled at the intimate gesture as a frisson of pleasure spiraled upward into her heart.

"My lovely one, I adore you." His dark green eyes laughed into hers. He picked up a tress of her red-gold hair and curled it about his fingers possessively. "You have the most wondrous hair I've ever seen, and all men who lay eyes on it must long to play with it like this. Lily, you enthrall me. Your loveliness haunts me. How will I ever leave you?" Charles kissed her eyelids. "I have an unquenchable thirst for you. When I see you, I have to come close. Then, when I'm close I have an uncontrollable desire to touch you. I long to touch you all over, here and here." He cupped his hand around her breast and caressed it gently. "Your voice and your laughter arouse me instantly. Your fragrance fills my senses until I can almost taste you."

* * *

When Lily awoke in the morning, she kept her eyes closed, savoring the dream, holding it close for a long time. Charles Curry truly was the man of her dreams. In his arms, she had never felt so warm, safe, and secure in her life. Slowly, inevitably, the dream began to evaporate, and like mist, it melted away. In its place a feeling of dread crept into her consciousness. She sighed heavily, knowing she must accept the fact that she was absolutely penniless. Movies were the business of make-believe; real life was very different.

Lily opened her eyes and saw that once again her surroundings had been transformed into the old west. She was lying in an iron bed and on her pillow lay a gold coin. "Oh heavens, I'm still dreaming." She closed her eyes for a minute, and when she opened them again, she was back in her own time. The gold coin however was still there. She sat up slowly and reached for the coin. "It's real! I'm not dreaming at all."

She examined the coin and to her amazement and delight she saw that it was a ten-dollar gold piece.

It had an eagle holding three arrows and the motto *In God We Trust.* "How on earth did this get here?" She gazed up at the ceiling, but saw no place from where it could have fallen. She jumped out of bed and ran to the door, thinking someone must have come into her room in the night, but she found the door securely locked, just as she had left it.

Lily turned the coin over and saw the head was Lady Liberty surrounded by thirteen stars. As she looked up, she saw the face of Abraham Curry in the painting and felt a strange connection. "It's a miracle!" she whispered.

She dressed carefully, choosing her best frock, a pale aqua silk. She put on her high heels that made her legs look extra-long and slim. She carefully placed the gold coin in her purse and left the hotel. "How will I spend it? I have so many choices."

On Virginia Street, she strolled toward the famous Reno Arch. She stopped to glance through the window of a coffee shop. *Should I buy breakfast?* Lily hesitated, loathe to part with the gold coin. *Perhaps I'll buy a new dress.* Further down the block she gazed in the window of a ladie's dress shop, almost giddy that she could spend the money on anything she fancied. She window-shopped jewelry stores, lingerie shops, and a place that showcased fancy hats as she strolled along in the sunshine. In the next block, she stopped and looked at a place that specialized in fancy Western garb and cowboy boots.

Lily's practical nature asserted itself. She had had an enjoyable morning, fantasizing about buying new clothes, but she knew without a doubt that she would go back to the casino, now that she had money to wager. Today, she felt extremely optimistic, as if Fortune was smiling on her.

Chapter Four

Inside the Riverside Casino, Lily made her way to the teller's cage to buy tokens. To her delight, the man in front of her was Charles Curry.

"Hello, Lily. Here to try your luck?"

"Yes, I need to buy tokens for the slot machines." She opened her purse and took out the gold coin.

Charles' eyes widened. "Lily, do you mind if I have a look at that coin?"

She felt a little defensive, as if she was in possession of something that didn't belong to her, but she hid her reluctance and handed it to Charles.

"Just as I thought, this is one of the coins my grandfather minted! See the date, 1874, and this CC is the Carson City mint mark. I collect these coins, Lily. I always check in with Mabel here at the casino; she keeps any silver or gold coins for me."

"That's amazing, Charles. There is a painting in my room of your grandfather, Abraham Curry. You look just like him."

"My partner's father, George Wingfield, and my grandfather were best friends. There are paintings of Abraham Curry in all Wingfield hotel rooms." He held up the gold coin. "Lily, I'll give you a hundred dollars for this."

"A hundred dollars? But it's only a ten-dollar coin," she pointed out.

"It's a collector's item, Lily. It would probably bring more than a hundred in an auction sale. Is it a deal?" Charles reached for his wallet.

"Why yes, thank you so much." She smiled in disbelief at the twenty-dollar bills he handed her. Lily gave one to Mabel and asked for tokens for the slot machines. "My luck is high at the moment, so I'm off to play the machines."

Charles laughed. "Good luck, Lily."

Before she went to the slots, she made her way to the coffee shop and bought a cheese sandwich and a glass of milk. She was almost faint from hunger and relished every bite.

Back in the crowded casino, Lily walked slowly along the wall that held the colorful slot machines, deciding which one to try first. "Of course, number 17. Why didn't I try that one before?" she murmured. She sat down and put a token in every slot, closed her eyes and pulled the lever. Suddenly, lights flashed, music played, and loud bells began to chime. Her eyes flew open. "I think I won."

People crowded about her. "You won the jackpot!" someone cried. Everyone began to cheer.

Lily was laughing with joy. "I can't believe it!"

Mabel, the cashier arrived, and close behind her was Charles Curry.

"Charles, I've won the jackpot–I've won a thousand dollars–I'm rich!"

"Lily, that's wonderful; you predicted your luck was high." Charles saw her face was alight with happy disbelief. *Sweet, innocent girl. She thinks a thousand dollars is a fortune.*

Mabel smiled at Lily. "If you follow me, miss, I will pay out your jackpot."

As Lily walked with Mabel and Charles, she smiled up at him. "It's my turn, Charles, will you join me for dinner tonight?"

"I'm sorry… Lily… I have a rule. I don't accept dinner invitations from ladies."

She stared at him in horror for one moment, then they both whooped with laughter.

* * *

For their dinner date, Charles chose to take her to the Trocadero Room that fairly dripped with Art Deco swankiness.

Lily's eyes sparkled. "Oh my heavens, this is just like a film set."

"I thought it a perfect place for a Hollywood actress."

Lily laughed. "I'm not really an actress. I'm more of a dancer."

They both ordered steak and salad, and laughed that their tastes were so similar. Charles ordered them champagne to celebrate Lily's good fortune. She smiled as she lifted her glass and Charles proposed a toast: "Here's to Lily London, a future Hollywood star."

Lily's smile faded and she said earnestly, "Oh, I'll never be a star."

"Why ever not?" he asked, bemused.

"To become a star, you have to be driven by ambition. Nothing else matters but stardom. They sacrifice everything to it, and as a result female movie stars become hard as flint! I could never be like that. When I first arrived at eighteen, I didn't know that, of course. I was innocent and starry-eyed, and liked to dance. But after working in films for two years, I've come to realize the competition is so fierce that women will stab each other in the back to get ahead in the business."

Charles nodded. "Sadly, you speak the truth."

"Now that I'm rich, I won't have to trek round the studios every day, begging for bit parts. I'll be able to explore other lines of work."

Charles lifted his glass. "Here's to a glorious future, whatever you choose." He watched her sip her champagne. "Tomorrow is your last day. Are you planning to try your luck again?"

"Gamble with my precious money? I wouldn't dream of wagering one dollar of it."

"In that case, why don't you let me show you around Carson City? I'll give you a tour of all the places that are said to be haunted."

"I can't think of anything I'd enjoy more. Thank you so much, Charles."

* * *

The following day, Charles Curry's Lincoln covered the twenty-five miles to Carson City in half an hour. Their first stop was the Governor's Mansion on Mountain Street. "It's said to be haunted by a woman in a white dress, who is always accompanied by a young girl. The two of them have been seen by countless people."

They got out of the car so that Lily could get a good look at the place. "It's a grand old house. I'd like to believe it's a devoted mother and her daughter who were so happy here, they come back to visit again and again."

Charles smiled. "That's a lovely thought. Come on across the street. This here is the Bliss Mansion. Various members of the wealthy Bliss family are often seen about the rooms of the house or standing in the back yard. They are said to appear and disappear at will."

"Have you ever seen them, Charles?"

"Not that I'm aware of. Come on, I'll show you the Edwards House, it's not far."

"This is another grand old home. Look at the lovely big bay windows."

"The housekeeper, Mrs. Maria Anderson, has been seen sitting in the bay windows. Rumor has it that she loved the piano, and to this day she always keeps it dusted."

Lily laughed. "I love these old legends, and I believe it's quite possible for a ghost to do things over and over." She didn't tell Charles, but last night Abraham Curry had come to her in a dream and told her that he had chosen her to become his grandson's wife. When she awoke this morning, there had been another ten-dollar gold coin on her pillow and she was totally convinced that it was Abraham Curry who was leaving them for her.

Charles drove down another street. "This is the Ferris House. It is said that whenever there is a wedding here, a ghostly bride from the past shows up to be one of the guests." He drove her to see a few more haunted houses and pointed out where the legendary Kit Carson had lived. Then he took her to the Mint Museum on North Carson Street. "You'll love this place."

"Oh, it's such a lovely building. Isn't this the legendary sandstone I've heard so much about?"

"Yes. Grandfather loved the sandstone. Wait until you see the inside."

Lily was fascinated by everything in the museum.

"This is a life-size replica of a Nevada ghost town. This is a mining camp, here's the newspaper office, and the assay office." He took her into the general store with its displays of old western merchandise, and finally the saloon with its bar, wooden stools and brass foot rail. Lily was delighted with the honky-tonk piano, the old-west furnishings, the antique whiskey bottles, and the brass spittoons. They even went to the basement of the museum to view the replica of a 19th-century gold mine.

* * *

On the way back to the car, Charles asked, "Would you like to see where I live, Lily?"

"Of course, I would." She blushed. "I thought you'd never ask."

"We passed my property on the drive here this morning. It's on the edge of the national forest, near Washoe Lake. It's a small ranch with enough room for a few horses."

"That sounds like paradise," she said wistfully.

He watched her eyes fill with wonder as she took in the lush landscape.

"I think I've fallen in love with Carson City."

I think I've fallen in love with you, Lily.

Charles parked the car in front of the ranch house. "Do you think you could give up Hollywood to live here, Lily?"

"Absolutely. In fact, I've decided not to return. Tomorrow, I intend to start looking for a job."

"In that case, I may be able to help you." He smiled and his eyes crinkled at the corners.

"That would be wonderful, but I don't want to–"

He put his finger to her lips to stop her words. "Please impose on me, Lily."

Her pulse began to race. He took her hand and led her into the house. The first thing she noticed was a portrait of Abraham Curry above the fireplace.

"Make yourself comfortable; I'll get us a cold drink."

Lily stood gazing up at Abraham's piercing green eyes. "You came to me in my dream last night," she whispered. "I know it was you who gave me the gold coins."

Charles set down the glasses and came to stand beside Lily. "My grandfather came to me also in my dream last night. He gave me some wonderful advice." He placed his hands on her shoulders and turned her to face him. "Lily, will you marry me?"

His green eyes searched her heart-shaped face, then slowly he drew her hand to his mouth and he kissed each fingertip. Lily's insides curled at the intimate gesture as a frisson of pleasure spiraled upward into her heart. He took possession of her mouth, just as her scream erupted, and kissed her until it turned into a sigh.

7

BURNING LOVE

A Burn Series Prequel

Crystal Perkins

Hot in the City

Afton

"Wake up, Afton. You need to help!"

"Help what?" I ask my aunt, trying to burrow deeper under my blanket.

"There's a fire. It's spreading."

Her words jolt me awake and I throw on my clothes before running from my room. I don't know how I'm able to help, but I know I can. It's a gift—or a curse. I haven't decided which one yet.

I don't have time to dwell on that as I jump into my car and drive toward the fire. I can feel it as well as see it and it makes it hard for me to breathe. Not just because the air is smoky but because I feel fire in my blood when I'm near it. Even cooking on our stove back at the farmhouse is uncomfortable. I can deal with being uncomfortable, though, because that's pretty much my life.

When I get as close as I can, I step away from the people with hoses, trying valiantly to fight the spreading blaze. Some in this town know my secret, but they protect me with a fierceness I'm not always sure I deserve. Sometimes I think it's because they don't want the media and government circus that outing me would bring. Other times, I know it's because the power I wield can save us on nights like tonight. I have no illusions it's just me their protecting, because I'm no one to this town, other than the girl who can make it rain.

Hiding in the alley between the bank and the general store, I cloak myself in the shadows and raise my hands to the sky. My call will be answered, of that I have no doubt. The only thing I can't control is the timing—yet. I'm working on harnessing the power I can bring, and I know with time I'll master it. Trouble is, I don't always have time. Like right now, when I need the water *right now*.

Come on. Come on. Please. There you are. Thank you.

The rain begins as a soft shower, before becoming a torrential downpour. I fight for control and for the first time, I have it. I move my hands as I communicate what I want with my mind. With the water focused on the fire alone, it's put out in minutes. I say a silent thank you to my elemental friend, and keep it going a little longer so it doesn't look unnatural. The exhaustion hits when I drop my hands to my side and I know I need to work more on controlling this power I have—before it destroys me.

* * *

Brock

I watch her, because how can I not? She's the most gorgeous girl I've ever seen, with her wild and curly hair, soft curves and a soft mouth I can't help but want to kiss. She's only in profile so I can't see her eyes, which is probably a good thing. I don't know if I'd survive seeing her full-on.

"What are you doing here?" my boss, Mat, asks.

Boss. I almost shake my head at that, because it's ridiculous. Once I got out from under my father's thumb, I didn't think I'd ever have someone else tell me what to do. My inheritance kicked in when I turned 21 and I was ready to do my own thing. Until the letter came. The letter from my grandfather, asking me to come to this small town in Nevada and learn to be a cowboy. If he'd been alive I could've asked him why this was so important. But he's not, and since I loved him more than anyone else on this Earth, I did what he asked. I'm here, I'm surviving the hard work, and I think I just found the girl of my dreams.

"I was going to help with the fire, but I wasn't needed."

"You saw nothing."

Oh, I saw something all right. "She brought the rain."

"We have freak rainstorms out here all the time. The city folk call it Global Warming."

He's lying and we both know it. I don't know how she did it, but the beauty with the wild hair brought the rain. She saved this town and I want to know more about her. No, I *need* to know. For now, I'll play along and keep this secret.

"That has to be it," I agree.

He searches my eyes and I force myself to look believable. I know it works when he nods.

"It is."

It's not, but I'm not going to get into it with him. I'd rather get into it with her and believe me, I will. I'm going to know that girl and learn how she did what she did. And then, I'll take her to bed. Because yeah, she may have brought the rain, but she's still hot as Hell.

I'm Still Standing

Afton

I slept half a day away after bringing the rain in the early hours of the morning, because controlling an element is no easy thing. At least I have a late shift at the diner today. Yeah, I work in the town diner like some cliché of a small-town girl who has no chance of leaving. It was either the diner or the grocery store. Some days, I'm not sure I made the right choice. Days like today.

I walk over to his table, because I have to. "Hello, Afton."

"Nick," I reply.

He looks me over, but not in a sexual way. It's like he's sizing me up and finding me lacking. Nothing new there—the mayor of our small town has always seemed to find me lacking.

"I want my usual."

"Got it."

I start to walk away, but he's not done with me yet. "How lucky we had that rainstorm last night. Funny that it only lasted such a short time and was just where we needed it to be."

"Not gonna complain about it," I tell him with a shrug.

"I'm sure you won't."

I force myself to maintain my smile and not shudder. There's something about the man that's always made me uncomfortable. It's like he's seeing into my soul and looking for a way to use what he finds against me. Well, he can just keep on looking.

I'm not an angel, but I'm a pretty good girl. I had good grades in school, I work hard—and yeah, I save my town whenever I can. If we had tracks through town instead of on the outskirts, I'd be on the wrong side of them when I sleep at night, which rubs some people wrong, even as they know they need Betty and me. But that's it. I'm not rich, but I'm also not bad. And I'm not about to turn to the dark side anytime soon.

* * *

Brock

Ranch work is no joke. I'm up before dawn tending to some animals, herding cattle during the day, and trying to sleep in a cabin at night. The cabin's nice, but the sounds of animals and not cars outside is not soothing to me. I don't live in a huge city, but it's big enough to have tall buildings and chain restaurants. I can eat here at the ranch but seeing the same people every single day is making me stir crazy, even after a couple of weeks.

That's why I find myself walking into the only diner in town tonight. It has nothing to do with finding out who the girl from last night was and knowing she works here. Nothing at all. I can almost believe that until I see her again.

Tonight, her hair is back in a ponytail with the curls flowing down her back. She's got on a tank top and a jean skirt along with boots on her feet. There's only one word I can think of to describe her right now—stunning. I'm literally stunned as I look at her.

She turns to face me, and *damn*. Those blue eyes are just... yeah. "You can have a seat anywhere you'd like, Cowboy."

Cowboy? Oh yeah, I still have my hat on. I pull it off, holding it in my hand as I blatantly stare at her. I can't help it. "Which is your section?"

"Oh, *City Boy*, it's not like that," she tells me, cocking a hip and placing her hand on it.

"Like what?"

"You don't get to come here, put a hat on your head and a checked shirt over your abs, and expect me to drop my panties for you."

At the sound of laughter, I turn around to see all the other patrons chuckling at my expense. Anger flares in my veins, because I've done nothing wrong. Yeah, I came in here hoping to meet her. And yeah, I'm more than a little intrigued by her. But, I didn't ask her to jump on my dick and go for a ride. I *wouldn't* do that—at least not before we had at least one date.

"I don't believe I asked you to drop anything, but I've suddenly lost my appetite."

Spinning on my own boot-clad heels, I shove the door open and storm outside. I'm not ready to get in my pickup, so I turn on the nearly deserted street and start walking. I haven't gone far when I hear boots moving fast behind me.

"Wait. I'm sorry," she says, grabbing my arm and turning me to her.

Even out of breath, she's still beautiful. Doesn't mean I'm not still mad. "You set out to embarrass me, so mission accomplished."

"You were hitting on me."

"Not yet, I wasn't."

"I don't sleep around. Nothing wrong with women who do, but I don't."

"Okay. I'll admit to wanting to ask you out after I saw you in the rain last night, but I wasn't going to force anything on you."

She draws in a sharp breath. "You saw me last night?"

"Yes."

She backs away slowly, like she's scared of me. "I have to go."

"I'm not going to tell anyone. I promise."

She hesitates for a moment before practically running back to the diner. I get that she has no reason to trust me or believe me, but I want her to. It shouldn't matter since I'm only here another month, yet it does.

<u>I Hear the Secrets That You Keep</u>

Afton

Growing up in this town has its perks, and knowing where the cabins at the dude ranch are is just one of them. Unfortunately, I don't know which one *he's* in. Luckily, I find him on my third peek into a window or I'd probably get reported as a Peeping Tom.

"Hello," I tell him when he opens the door.

He's shirtless, because of course he is. And yeah, he has abs for days. Months. Years. Just yum.

"My eyes are up here," he tells me, and I don't miss the tilt of his lips once I force my eyes up.

"Should've put a shirt on before you opened the door if you didn't want me to look."

He crosses his arms over an impressive set of pecs, highlighting even better biceps. "Didn't know it was you."

"Not checking your peephole, City Boy?"

"My name's Brock. You know, just in case you want to use it sometime."

"I'll consider it."

"Have you considered telling me your name too?"

"Oh. Afton."

"What can I do for you on this fine evening, Afton?" he asks, leaning against the doorframe, which causes his jeans to sit a little lower on his hips. Damn.

"I wanted to talk to you."

"So, talk."

"May I come inside."

"You're more than welcome to *come* inside."

I roll my eyes and turn to walk away. "This was a bad idea."

"Wait," he tells me, reaching out to touch my arm. "I was being an ass. Please come inside and talk."

I want to flip him off and keep walking, but I came here for a reason. "Let's talk."

* * *

Brock

I know what she wants to talk about and I also know I want to get to know her better. Somehow, I have to turn one topic into the other. I'm just not sure how to do it yet.

"What exactly is it you thought you saw?"

"Straight to the point, huh?" I joke, but she doesn't smile. "Oh-kay. I saw you bring the rain."

"Bring the rain?"

"You raised your hands up and it started raining shortly after."

"I was praying."

I shake my head. "No. As soon as you dropped your arms, it stopped. You somehow controlled it."

"I can assure you, I wasn't in complete control."

"But you admit you brought it?"

"Yeah. I mean, you saw it so there's no point in hiding it. You promised to keep my secret and I'm holding you to that."

"Absolutely. I'd love to know more. More about the water and more about you."

"I need to sit down for this," she says, dropping into the chair by the bed. I sit on the bed itself.

"I'm listening."

"My mother died during childbirth and my father—well, who knows where he was? My aunt took me in and raised me. She has a small farm, but it thrives. No matter what, her crops all come to fruition and she stays afloat. The whole town thrives, in fact."

"I've noticed."

I have. This ranch, along with the other ranches and farms here all turn a profit. While they're not rich, everyone here seems comfortable.

"I don't know if it's her, because I've never asked. I don't know if I really want the answer to that question," she admits.

"I get it."

She looks at me for a moment, a thoughtful look on her face. "I think you do."

"My grandpa was the most stand-up guy I knew, but my dad? Well, I don't want to know how he's managed to turn the billions he inherited into even more."

"Sometimes it's better to stay innocent."

"Are you innocent?" I ask.

She laughs. "I'm not a virgin, if that's what you're asking."

I shrug. "I kinda was."

"I know."

"Mind-reader too?"

"Nope, just water."

"Tell me."

"It started when I was a little girl, but I didn't realize what I was doing. I wanted it to rain one day and it did. A torrential downpour I wasn't prepared for, but the rain came. And then I fell into the swimming hole and the water seemed to lift me to the surface. I didn't know how to swim yet and I would've drowned, but I swore it felt like hands pushing me to the top. Later, it was water jumping from one of my hands to the other when I was playing in the bathtub. By the time I was a teen, I could turn water into waves when I wanted to learn to surf and cause the water fountains to splash up into the faces of the mean girls when they went for a drink."

"So, you didn't always use your power for good?"

"Mean girls, Brock. Keep up. I balanced the scales a little."

"I've never been turned on by a vigilante before."

"Perv."

"I'll own it. And I'll keep your secret."

"Thanks. There have been fires in the last year I've been able to put out, so that's what I focus on now."

"The guys say they don't know how those fires have been starting. It looks to them like there was nothing around that could've started them."

"I believe that too. Something else is going on here and I'm going to find out what it is."

"How old are you?" I blurt out.

"19."

"I'm 21."

"Good for you."

"Go out with me tomorrow."

"I do have the day off."

"Is that a yes?"

"Yes."

Hold Me Now

Afton

It's been two weeks since I agreed to that first date with Brock and things are going better than I expected them to. We've both always known he was leaving in two more weeks, so things have been light and fun. I haven't even let him kiss me on the lips yet. Tonight, I will. We're going to the town carnival and I want to hold his hand

and kiss him—maybe even more. He's still leaving and I'm still staying, but it just feels right.

An hour later, I start to re-think things. He didn't come to pick me up when he said he would and my calls keep going to voicemail. I gave up ten minutes ago and drove myself to the town square. It's not as fun being in a dress and make-up without him, but I'm not going to just wait around all night until he shows up.

"Looking good," one of the other cowboys says and I flip him off.

Yeah, no. Not waiting, but not looking for someone else either.

My eyes search for Brock, hoping beyond hope I don't see him here with someone else. I have no reason to believe he'd do that, but I look anyway.

"Missing your date, Afton?"

I turn to the mayor, because my aunt raised me to be respectful. "How do you know I have a date?"

"You and that Johnston boy have been inseparable these last two weeks. Pity to get so close to someone who's going to be leaving you behind soon."

"Who's to say I'm not leaving with him?" I challenge him.

The words are out too fast for me to stop them. I've thought about it, but I haven't said them out loud. Not to Brock, not to myself—not to anyone.

He smirks. The creep actually smirks at me. "You belong here. Here is where you will stay."

"That's not for you to decide."

I storm past him, determined to not engage any further with him. He makes me feel unsettled and I'm already an emotional mess right now. I don't need the added stress.

A young girl bumps into me, spilling her water on my hand. She apologizes, but it's not her I hear or see in front of me. I see Brock, half in and half out of the swimming hole. It's like he's suspended there, although I see nothing binding him.

"*Help!*"

"Brock?" I think the word in my head, because I don't need people thinking I talk to myself.

"*Afton? Something's holding me here. I can't move.*"

"I'm coming for you. Hold on."

Turning to go, I run right back into the mayor. "Excuse me."

"Where are you rushing off to, Afton?"

"None of your business."

"If you're going to the swimming hole or your aunt's farm, it is indeed my business."

The farm? "What are you saying?"

"Betty was always too kind-hearted. Helping these people who don't deserve it. You on the other hand understand that your power can be fun too."

"I don't know what you're talking about."

"I watched your great-great-great-great grandmother die at the stake. There might be another 'great' or two in there, but you get the picture. I watched the flames burn her as she looked into my eyes."

"What?"

"She was a powerful witch, but not powerful enough to save herself."

"How would you have been there?"

"Because I *am* powerful enough to survive. And because as a man, I had more power than she did in the community. I always hold all the power."

"Not over me, you don't."

"But dear daughter, I do."

I suck in a breath and look him over from head to toe. "No."

"Yes. Your mother craved the power she knew we could have together. Too bad I didn't need her once I had you."

"You don't have me. You will *never* have me, even if what you're saying is true."

"Really? Because I hold the lives of your beloved aunt and your would-be lover in my hands."

He cups his hands and holds them up to me. It's like looking at a split-screen video. One side is Brock in the water and the other is Aunt Betty suspended over a fire. No.

"Come with me and rule by my side, and I will free them both."

"How do I know you'll keep you word?"

"You don't."

Before he can say another word, I run. I run to my old pickup truck and race to the farm. I'm beginning to care about Brock, but my aunt raised me. I have to save her and then I'll try to save him.

"I understand."

I forgot about our connection. "I'm sorry."

"Don't be. I'll hold on here for as long as I can. Save your aunt."

* * *

Brock

The water is getting colder as I slide lower into it. It was only an inch at a time when I first connected with Afton, but it's more and more every minute now. I know he's going to kill me. She had a choice to make and she made the one she had to. I'm trying to hope she can make it to me before it's too late, but I have to be honest with myself. My last breaths will take place in this water. My only regret is that I didn't get to kiss her like she deserves to be kissed.

"Hold on, Brock. We're on our way."

I can't answer her as my mouth is now under water. Breathing through my nose isn't something I'll ever take for granted again if I make it out of here. *If.*

I hear gravel flying as a car comes down the road right before my ears slip below the surface of the water. My lungs are fighting for air that isn't here and I'm dying.

"You are not dead yet, Brock. Fight."

I feel light on my face and open my eyes to see a woman under the water with me. She looks like Afton, only older. There's a glow around her and I have no doubt this is her mother. Her *dead* mother. Other glowing women come to stand behind her. They're dressed in all manner of clothing, from all different time periods. I should be afraid, but I'm not.

"Fight. She is coming for you. You must fight today—and you must fight in the future when she comes to you. You will be apart for many years, but when she needs you, fight for her. With her. Promise me, Brock."

"I promise."

I say it in my mind, but I know she hears it when her image dissolves in front of me. I feel hands pulling at the invisible ties binding me and then I'm pushed to the surface. I flail my arms as I take large gulps of air.

"Brock!"

I turn to see Afton and her aunt on the bank on the water. Afton dives in and surfaces next to me, placing her arms around me as the water seems to lift us out of it and onto the ground. I fall to my knees

113

before looking up at the woman in front of me.

"You must be Betty," I tell her, holding out my hand. "You look like your sister."

She sucks in a sharp breath. "She was here with you."

"What? My mother?"

"Yeah. Her and a bunch of other women appeared to me underwater. She asked me for a promise and then they helped me to the surface."

"Only a man with a pure heart can see the ancestors."

"Um, okay."

"What did she make you promise?" Afton demands.

"To help you when we meet again."

I don't tell her I'm supposed to fight for her, because I now know I'm leaving here without her. When we re-connect, I'll tell her how I've loved her since the day I saw her in the rain, but not now. Now, we have to go our separate ways.

"Meet again?"

Betty nods. "You must go and hide, Afton. Disguise yourself as best you can and become someone new. Do not use your powers and do not dress as you do now. I cannot bear to ask you to cut your hair, but everything else about you must change."

"I can't leave you! *He* is still here. He'll try to kill you again."

"Try, yes. But he will not succeed. If the ancestors are here, they will stay and protect me. I feel it. I feel *them*."

"Brock?"

"I know you have to go. It's what has to happen."

"Tonight. You will have this one night where you are protected. Go and make the most of it." Betty tells us.

I'm not going to argue. "Let's go."

<u>The End of the World as We Know It</u>

Afton

It's too much. Tonight is too much and not enough all at once. Brock brackets my face in his hands the moment we're inside his cabin. His mouth descends on me just like I've imagined it would. We kiss softly at first and then it becomes more.

More lips, more teeth, and more tongue until our hands are exploring each other's bodies with abandon. There's no time for candles and flower petals, but I know now I'm not a girl who needs that from the man she loves.

Yes, I love him. Yes, it's too soon. And no, I don't care. I won't tell him tonight because I have to leave in the morning, but it's true.

The next few hours are lost in a tangle of limbs, mouths, and other body parts. I'm both sated and hungry for more at the same time. Brock must feel the same way, because he takes my body over and over again. I've never felt anything like this with anyone else, and I know I never will again. Not until we're back together. I mourn the loss of him as the sun comes up, but I know this is what we both need to do.

* * *

Brock

I feel Afton slipping out of bed, and I reach out a hand to stop her. "One more kiss."

"Just one and then I have to leave."

"For now."

"Yes, for now."

I kiss her sweetly, pouring all of my love into it. "We will be together again."

"So I've been told."

"I believe her."

"And I believe you."

"I need you to know that even if I'd never made that promise, I would always be there when you need me."

"I believe that too."

"Stay safe."

"I plan to."

"One more thing," I say, reaching into the nightstand.

"There's no time."

"Not that, dirty girl. This."

I hold out the watch to her. It's covered in diamonds and completely ostentatious.

"Um."

"My grandfather bought this with his first million. He never wore it after the day he bought it. When I was little, I found it and he told me he thought he'd needed it to show the world he was

115

important, but he didn't. Even though he didn't need it, he kept it and when I saw him for the last time, he told me I'd know who I needed to give it to."

"I can't take it."

"You have to. He was the person I loved more than anything in the world—and now, that's you."

"Brock."

"I know I shouldn't say it and I planned not to, but it's true."

"I love you too."

"Take the watch and come to me when you need me. I'll be waiting."

"I can't ask you to do that."

"You didn't."

She slides the watch onto her wrist, kisses me one more time, and then she's gone. We'll find our way back to each other and then we'll be together forever. I've got two more weeks on this ranch before I go home and I'm going to spend as much of it with Betty as possible. When the time comes, I need to be ready to help and fight to the death for Afton if necessary. That's now my mission in life.

8

THE COWBOY AND THE FAIRY GODMOTHER

Eileen Dreyer

1937

Emily Jackson loved trains. She enjoyed watching the scenery, sleeping to the sway of the car, sitting at the linen-covered table in the cafe to enjoy a dinner served by white-coated waiters. Before Matt had became so famous, she'd even enjoyed interacting with the other passengers.

She didn't, however, enjoy the train that was taking her to Reno.

It wasn't the train's fault, or the staff, who worked so hard to make her comfortable, whether they recognized her or not. It wasn't that the trip was too long. Only from Los Angeles, after all, not New York. But the train to Reno tended not to be a happy train. From where she sat in the first class car, Emily could hear the sniffles, the sighs, and sometimes even sobs from other seats. This was the Divorce Train, and most of the people on it regretted the ride.

For Emily's part, she was ready for this trip. If she were honest with herself, she'd been ready for five years now. Where the other women felt grief and anger and disbelief, she just felt a grinding weariness.

"Mrs. Shephard, ma'am," the porter said, bending over her with perfect deference, "can I help you with your luggage?"

She looked up, surprised to realize they were slowing. Buildings passed, the rather shoddy, unkempt kind that lined railroad tracks. At a crossing, several cars and a beat-up truck full of vegetables waited for the flashing red lights to change. Beyond, Emily saw the dusty brown desert spread all the way to the mountains on the horizon.

"Thank you, Sam." She didn't even have to gesture to the Goyard luggage that already sat in a tidy pile by the door. "Everything else is in the baggage car."

Six weeks in the desert. She sighed. She would have been much happier surviving this purgatory in Wyoming or Montana, not in an over-priced dude ranch with a hundred other women awaiting divorce. She was too long-past talked and smiled out. She wanted respite.

Well, at least she'd have Misty for company.

Gathering her gloves and purse, Emily quickly checked her make-up. She grimaced. She didn't have to do that anymore. No one's reputation would suffer because she didn't have on lipstick. No cameras would flash in her eyes, no reporter ask breathy questions about her Chanel suit or sigh-worthy husband.

Her soon to be ex-husband who had finally formalized his infidelities by running off with his latest leading lady.

"Someone pickin' you up, ma'am?" Sam asked.

"The Flying M E is sending a car," she said, watching Reno gather around her.

Sam nodded, needing no explanation for that either. Emily was sure he was quite familiar with that car. Everyone she knew in Hollywood stayed at the Flying M E for their divorce.

The train was sliding into the station now, a gaggle of people waiting on the platform. Emily noticed one in particular, a tall, rangy cowboy in battered Stetson, battered jeans and battered boots. For just a second, her heart clenched with longing. Oh, if only she had any energy left for dreaming anymore. He was a real ranchman like those back home, whose elbows and knees were worn and whose face was weathered and jaw-solid.

When Matt played a cowboy, he was pressed and coiffed and sprayed with just a little water to make it look like he'd been sweating in the sun. This man was dusty, his chestnut hair a little too long and his stride wide and strong. A real person. And when was the last time she'd met one of those?

It was too late, though, she thought, dropping her compact into her Jean Patou bag and snapping it shut. Five years too late, really. Matt had left her with no more room in her dreams for men. Even if that man looked like a cowboy who walked like he knew the worth of work. She just wanted peace. She wanted to remember what it was to be happy. At least not miserable.

"He is pretty, isn't he?" she heard behind her.

Emily turned and almost laughed. "Pardon?"

There was a tiny, white-haired woman in tweed approaching up the aisle, her eyes crinkled with delight, her thin lips curved, her step springy. She motioned to where the cowman outside walked along with the train. "The cowboy. I sure wouldn't mind tangoing with him, if you know what I mean."

Now Emily did laugh. She turned back in time to see the man lift his head as if looking for someone on the stopping train. Chills unaccountably chased down her spine at the flash she got of his eyes, a pale blue the color of morning snow on the Nevadas, the abrupt angled shadows of cheek and chin beneath a low-pulled Stetson.

Kiss me, she thought.

Jiminy. Her breath stuttering in her chest. She was blushing. He wasn't the most beautiful man in the world. She'd been swimming in those for the last seven years and hadn't once thought that. But he was... he was...

"Solid as the Rock of Gibraltar," the old woman unaccountably said, as if she'd heard Emily's thoughts. "Wouldn't you like him for your very own?"

He came to a halt right in front of their window at the same moment the train made its final shuddering stop. Emily couldn't pull her gaze away from him, standing so solid and grounded before her, craggy as the mountains she loved, easy as ocean breezes.

"I'm sure he's lovely," she said, smiling even though even that suddenly hurt all over again, "but I've just sworn off men. Completely."

That softened the little woman's smile 'til it seemed to gleam in the shady car. "I can't say as I blame you," she said with a nod. "You've had a rather rough time of it."

Emily flinched. She should have expected that. She had been splashed across Louella Parsons's column for the last six months as rumors grew about Matt and his leading ladies, especially since Louella seemed to blame her.

"I'd recognize you anywhere," the little lady said, patting Emily on the arm. "Matt Shepherd's beautiful wife who's donated so much of her time to the Red Cross. Your photos don't do you justice, my dear, even in that beautiful peach satin dress you wore to the Oscars."

Emily almost sighed. So much for a little fantasy. Not Emily Shephard, but Emily Jackson, all alone and and on her own adventure for the first time in her life, depending on no man who would just disappoint her again.

But she was Emily Shephard, wife of the movie star who regularly vied with Cary Grant and Errol Flynn for handsomest man in Hollywood. Inspiration for more fantasies than the word Hollywood itself.

"Yes," she said because it was expected. "The dress was pretty, wasn't it?"

And carefully folded away into the trunks and boxes that held her old life.

The little woman patted her again. "It isn't fair."

Emily shrugged. "Is it ever?"

"You were a good wife to him," the old woman stated, as if Emily needed defense. "He's a fool."

Her smile was rueful. "I know."

"And from what I've heard, you're even the one who taught him to ride."

Emily gave the oft-repeated answer. "We taught each other."

Ten-year-olds set loose in the foothills of the Medicine Bow Mountains. Inseparable through the years until a second-rate director got lost and saw Matt on a horse.

The doors to the train opened just as the little woman pointed out the window. "I imagine you'd like to escape that lot, too."

Emily whipped around again and groaned. Oh, murder! They'd found her. Suits rumpled, fedoras pushed back on their heads, a pack of reporters jostled each other for position, cameras poised to click her first step off the train.

This was the last thing she needed right now. She should never have listened to Paulette Goddard when she'd said that the train was the way to go.

"Yes," she said with growing dread. "I would dearly love to miss all that."

"Well," the little lady said with a delighted chortle. "What are fairy godmothers for? Let's head out the coach car."

And before either Emily or Sam could protest, the little woman grabbed her wrist and was dragging her down the car toward the back door.

"Wait!" Emily protested. "I have to tip Sam."

"No time. I'll take care of it."

How? The train would start moving in about ten minutes.

"What's your name?" Emily asked, stumbling along behind the surprisingly fast old lady. Narrow skirts and Spanish heels simply weren't made for a getaway.

"My name?" The little woman grinned over her the shoulder. "Why, Merryweather, of course." As if that should have rung some bell.

They reached the back of the car and pushed through to the next. And at the far end of that emptying car, finally, the little woman pulled to a stop. A large, noisy family was crowding through the doorway ahead of them, effectively blocked the view to–or from–the press.

Emily tried to take her hand back. "Thank you. I–"

But the little woman turned on her.

"If you had any wish at all," she said, not letting go, "what would it be?"

Oddly, it seemed important. "A wish? What could I wish for?"

After all, she would still have wealth. At least her lawyer had made sure of that. She had some friends who still lived back home. She was still a nurse, so she could keep busy. She had loved her job, especially those years when she had helped Matt achieve his dream. They had been such a team...

Enough of that. Miss Merryweather still held her hand, and the family was pushing off the train ahead of them in a chattering, laughing mass.

"What do you wish for?" the woman clarified. "Right now."

Emily tried to get a look past the family. Beyond them, two women were passing, handkerchiefs up to shield tears, one holding a little blond girl by the hand. The sight of that bouncing child squeezed Emily's heart, even so long after it had surrendered to the inevitable. And there at the far end of the platform, the press still waited. Emily's stomach dropped all over again.

"I wish I could disappear," she said out loud.

The old woman nodded, as if it had been the right answer. "Do you like the mountains?"

"What?" Emily asked, blinking. "Yes, of course."

"Well then, that's all right then."

And before Emily could say anything more, even as the porter held his hand out to help her off the train, the old lady toppled right off the top step and landed with a hollow crack on the concrete. And Emily swore she heard her mutter, "The things I do for my job" as she fell.

For a precious moment, Emily could only stand there frozen, as that plump little body seemed to wedge itself underneath the wheels of the train. Then she turned to the porter and gave him a push. "Tell them to hold the train! Tell them now!"

It only took one look at the crumpled form beneath him for the porter to nod and run back up the train. Emily climbed down and did her best to kneel by the prostrate woman, in a skirt that was far too narrow. Little Mrs. Merryweather was lying curled on her side on the concrete, one leg wedged right under a wheel, her little cloche hat shoved over her right ear and her purse skidding against a trash can. Her stockings were torn and one shoe off. A Mary-Jane, Emily noticed, and wondered how on earth the old woman could have ended up in such a way after only falling off two train steps.

And then she saw the blood.

"I need some help!" she called, completely forgetting the press as she bent far over to try to get a better assessment.

"Mrs. Merryweather." she said, leaning over her back.

The little woman didn't move. Emily reached to check her pulse to see that her left wrist was bent in the wrong place. She reached for the other wrist instead and breathed a sigh of relief. Mrs. Merryweather's heartbeat was strong and steady. Leaning closer, Emily saw that the blood was streaming from a ragged laceration over the little lady's left eye. She reached for her own purse.

"Can I help you, ma'am?" she heard just over her.

"Yes, please. Someone needs to call an ambulance—"

She looked up and froze. The cowboy. Oh, sweet lord, he was even more handsome up close, all angles and strength. And he smelled like horses and fresh air–like her personal fantasy. She actually felt a shiver race through her, head to curling toes.

Worse, he seemed to freeze just as solidly, bent toward her, his hat shading those ghostly eyes, his mouth gaping just a little. She thought maybe he wasn't breathing either.

"Kiss me," she mumbled.

He frowned at her. "Ma'am?"

She blinked, blushed. "Oh! An ambulance. Mrs. Merryweather here fell."

"Is that Miz Merryweather?" he asked, looking down. 'Why, Miz Merryweather," he said, kneeling across from Emily, "what have you gone and done?"

At that, almost as if by magic, the little old lady's eyes popped open. "That you, Joe?"

Emily stared. "You know each other?"

Joe's grin was bashful enough to win the Gary Cooper Award. "Yes ma'am, that we do. I was comin' to pick Fizz Merryweather up at the train."

Mrs. Merryweather harrumphed. "Just Merryweather. I've told you, Joe. It's all right, though. I have your horse."

Emily was staring again. "She got you a horse?"

"Special horse, she says, that'll change my life."

Emily shook her head. "Must be some horse."

He was still grinning. "Better be. Spent all my savings on him."

Emily kept thinking this was all going to make sense in a minute. There was Joe, removing his stetson and laying it next to the train, and Mrs. Merryweather now patting him on the arm with her good hand, the two of them smiling as if they'd reunited in her parlor.

"Wait 'til the two of you meet," she was telling him with that impish smile. "You'll be glad I went all this way for him."

"How far did you go?" Emily found herself asking as she reached for her purse.

Mrs. Merryweather giggled. "You have no idea."

Emily felt more and more disoriented. The cowboy–Joe–was grinning as if everything was wonderful now that he knew she'd gotten him a horse.

An old lady in a tweed suit and Mary Janes.

And darn it, if she didn't find him completely charming. It just wasn't fair.

The only thing she could think to do was revert to her training.

"Oddest horse dealer I've ever met." She shook her head. "We have other problems, er…" She looked up, lifted an eyebrow at the cowboy.

"Joe," he said, turning his smile on her. "Joe Matthews."

She couldn't help but smile back. "Emily Shephard." They nodded to each other, and Emily was sure her own smile was a shy as a schoolgirl's. It was absurd, but she couldn't seem to help it. She still wanted him to kiss her.

"Will you help me get Mrs. Merryweather clear of the wheels?" she asked. "I don't trust the train."

She should have anticipated it. Joe picked Mrs. Merryweather up as easily as if she were a child, his actions gentle and patient, lowering her back to the concrete once they were a safe distance from those deadly wheels. Then he tucked her skirt back down by her ankles to make sure her legs were covered. Emily hated this. How could her heart ache so hard just from an act of kindness?

And then he smiled at her, as if it was his greatest pleasure to follow her lead. Worse yet, he was smiling as if she were just an attractive stranger. His eyes weren't knowing or fawning or sneering as if he recognized her name. And he still smiled as if he were delighted to meet her.

Oh, lord, she was getting into deep water.

Trying to cover her distraction, Emily looked around for something to use to cushion Mrs. Merryweather's head on the concrete. She finally whipped off her white wool beret and tucked it under the silvery hair.

"There," she said. "Now all I need is a splint. A magazine, maybe. And your kerchief, Joe."

"Oh, your hat," Mrs. Merryweather protested, getting the white wool all bloody.

Emily grinned. "It was a gift from Matt," she confided, reaching into her purse to pull out her own handkerchief. "As good a use as any I had for it."

"Here," Joe said, pulling off a faded red kerchief from his throat to expose the sheen of sweat in the notch. Toe-curling all over again.

"Joe is starting his own ranch," the little woman said brightly as Emily pressed her handkerchief to the head laceration. "Isn't that lovely? In Wyoming."

"Want me to splint her wrist?" he asked. "I'm used to it."

Emily couldn't help but grin. "So am I. I'm a nurse."

"The perfect person to live out there isolated on a ranch," Mrs. Merryweather piped up. "Don't you think, Joe?"

Joe's nod was actually slow and thoughtful. "Probably would."

And then without asking, he took Emily's place and pressed her handkerchief.

"What's your ranch like?" Emily asked as she checked Mrs. Merryweather over for other breaks of any kind.

"Sweet little tract of land," he said. "Backs up to the Tetons. It was my granddad's."

He was smiling down at Mrs. Merryweather, his words soothing as he staunched the bleeding.

Emily looked up to see an almost reverent look on Joe's face as he spoke of the ranch. She was sure she had something intelligent to say; something bright and witty, and decidedly not that suddenly she wanted nothing more than to follow Joe to Wyoming. Certainly not that she wanted him to treat her as gently as this little old woman with his broad, strong hands and sky-bright eyes. All she could manage was, "Then why are you here?"

"Savin' to fix the place up. Worked the dude ranches."

Hopefully not the Flying M E. She didn't think she could survive that.

She managed a nod. "And Mrs. Merryweather is your... er, horse trader?"

It was Mrs. Merryweather who giggled. "No, dear. I told you. I'm a fairy godmother."

Emily shot Joe a look, but he just shrugged. "Uh huh. How does your head feel now, ma'am?"

"Everything will be fine. Just wait a minute."

"Well, we still need to get you splinted. Maybe we could ask—"

But before she could finish, a cold nose shoved into the back of her neck, making her squeak. She whipped around to find herself looking up into the dark liquid eye of the most beautiful gray filly she'd ever seen.

"What are you doing here?" she demanded.

"Is that my horse?" Joe asked in tones of reverence.

"No," Emily said, reaching up for the bridle. "This is my horse. Misty, how on earth did you get out?"

125

Which was, of course, when she heard thudding feet from the far baggage car. "Damn horse!" a voice yelled.

Emily couldn't help but grin as she stroked her girl's nose. "Have you been misbehaving?"

"She got you a horse, too?" Joe asked, obviously confused.

Emily smiled at him. "No, Misty came with me. I raised her from a foal."

Joe's eyes widened. "She's a beauty. You obviously know good horseflesh."

"Yes," she admitted without blushing. "I do."

Mrs. Merryweather chuckled. "Emily here plays polo, Joe."

Something the old woman had undoubtedly learned from the magazines. Well, Emily wasn't going to apologize for it. Or doing stunt riding for some of the actresses on Matt's films. It had been the only fun she'd had out there.

"Polo?" he asked, looking just a bit suspicious.

She refused to back down. "Polo. This is my favorite pony."

"So that is Erin's Misty Morn," Mrs. Merryweather said, sounding as if she'd met an old friend.

Emily whipped around on her. "How do you know?" She never used her formal name.

The old woman chuckled, which somehow didn't seem odd with her lying on concrete, with Joe holding a handkerchief to her head. "Well, do you think I'd pair Joe's stallion with anybody else? Oh, the babies they're going to make."

"What?" both Joe and Emily demanded at once.

Emily looked over to see Joe staring at her, obviously as unacquainted with Mrs. Merryweather's plan as Emily.

Just about at the same moment another voice yelled. "Loose horse!"

"Remind me not to use this train again," Emily murmured, still caught in the pale snow blue of Joe's eyes.

He grinned, and she thought she could easily fall right into that smile.

Kiss me. I mean it. Just once. Just so I know that kind of tingle all the way to my toes.

And then another horse trotted right up to them and nudged Misty in the side. Another gray, as pale as gloaming mist, with the same black mane and tail as Misty, who seemed to find him just as attractive as Emily found his owner. Emily swore her horse dipped her head and gave that stallion a coy, come-hither look.

"I assume this is his horse?" Emily asked, checking back with Joe to find herself matching bemused grins. Mrs. Merryweather was cooing as if the horses were puppies.

As for the horses, they turned as one and seemed to be assessing the scene. More odd even, nobody seemed to notice.

"There you are, Gray," Mrs. Merryweather chirped, struggling to sit up. "Are you ready to meet your new partners? Help me up, Joe."

"Are you sure that's wise?" Emily asked.

"Of course. I'll be perfectly fine in a minute." Once she was sitting up, she waved at the gray stallion. "Now, then. Graymist, your greetings, please."

Emily swore that horse knew just what she was saying. "Bloody hell," she whispered. Because just then, he dipped his sleek head and whuffled as if in greeting, his black mane swishing down to touch Emily's shoulder.

For a moment she couldn't look away from the two horses, side by side, each sleek and bright-eyed, ears cocked forward and bodies resting against each other as if they had known each other a long time. As if they were meant to stand together. Oh, jiminy, she thought. They would make beautiful babies.

"All a fairy horse needs," Mrs. Merryweather said, "is respect and purpose. And a lovely large land to roam. Graymist and Misty Morn will be perfect. They just need you two to see your way."

Emily couldn't stop staring at the old woman. Then she looked over to assess Joe's reaction, expecting to see him just as bemused. But he wasn't looking at Mrs. Merryweather. He wasn't looking at the horses. He was looking at her.

Joe was on his feet, chestnut hair gleaming, his eyes pale as Misty's coat. Around them the noise seemed to echo from far away. Emily's heart raced. She felt the oddest melting in her belly, as if the ice that had protected her these last years was suddenly melting. She felt breathless with possibility, and she had no idea how to handle that.

She'd never had this reaction before to anyone, and she had shared dances with Clark Gable and Cary Grant, had sat alongside David Niven and Douglas Fairbanks at polo matches. They'd been friends, acquaintances; nothing more. Someone to smile at and share stories of the more absurd people they'd run across during their forays into the land of fantasy.

This hadn't even happened with Matt. Matt had been her friend, her escape from a fractious family, her partner in adventure. Marriage had simply been the next logical step, not a fairy tale.

Not this. Not kiss me before I perish this.

"Oh, it's all so perfect," Mrs. Merryweather chortled. "One of my best plans ever, if I must say myself."

"Your plans?" Emily echoed,

"Why yes. I knew if it looked like I needed help you two would converge right on the spot. I was right. Wait til I tell the girls."

Emily almost believed it, that she'd been given a chance to simply step out of her life and into a new one with the wave of an old woman's hand. That she could be given the gift of a dependable man, a kind man, a gentle man, a man who curled her toes. And then, because that wasn't the way life worked, one of the passengers stepped forward.

"You said you needed a splint," the middle-aged woman said, her voice breathless, her eyes huge. "You can use my magazine."

And there it was. Emily's picture in that peach satin dress splashed across the front of Photoplay right alongside a shot of Matt in his tux and the headline WHAT MORE COULD SHE WANT? She knew the minute Joe Manion saw the magazine, read the headline, recognized the photo.

The light in his eyes winked out. His smile died. He looked like he'd caught her in a lie.

* * *

Joe Manion felt like a fool.

He'd started to believe the old woman's fairy tales. He'd seen himself riding the range on that stunning gray cow pony and standing alongside as that filly birthed the first generation of prime Flying M horses. He'd even seen it with Emily Shephard standing beside him.

Fool.

He should have known better. He was far too familiar with the women who came to Reno on the divorce train. He knew how many of them treated the six weeks forced residency. Not a few had invited him to share their sentence. Cocktails on the veranda, gambling in the evenings, trail rides by day and a different kind of horseplay at night.

And there was no question he would have enjoyed that horseplay with Emily Shephard.

Even though the boss forbade it, there were ways around that and the kind of women who had the money to wait out their divorce decrees in comfort.

Joe dreamed of an honest woman, a helpmate who wouldn't mind the isolation of the mountains in winter and thrived on hard work. A woman who knew how to laugh and when to cry, and who yearned to hold her own child in her arms. He'd let that dreaming get out of hand. It had prevented him from seeing the truth right in front of his eyes. All he'd been able to think from the minute he'd seen her on that train was that he wanted to kiss her in the worst way.

"Joe Manion," Mrs. Merryweather snapped, getting to her feet. "You stop that right now."

He didn't look down at her. He couldn't take his eyes off the woman who was even more beautiful than her picture in a movie magazine. He'd seen her right away, of course, that sassy red hair glowing inside the train car as they'd pulled in. The bright intelligence and unfussy competence. The startling green eyes that tilted up at the corners just a little, and lithe body so well framed in that designer dress.

He should have recognized money the minute he'd seen it. He should have recognized Matt Shephard's famous wife who played polo with Spencer Tracy's wife. But Mrs. Merryweather had distracted him.

Mrs. Merryweather who was on her feet, standing on one shoe and glaring up at him.

"Are you sure this is wise?" Emily was asking the old woman.

Mrs. Merryweather reached up to pat her cheek. With her left hand. That didn't look so crooked all of a sudden. "You are a dear. Of course it's wise. That's what I'm known for."

Joe was finally staring at her instead of her young friend.

Mrs. Merryweather looked completely uninjured. He looked down at the handkerchief he still held in his hand. Snowy white, not a drop of blood. He looked over to see Mrs. Shephard picking up her un-bloody beret.

"What the Sam Hill did you just do?" he demanded.

Mrs. Merryweather tsked. "Language, dear. There are ladies present."

129

Joe was starting on a headache.

"It seems," Mrs. Shephard was saying to the lady holding out the magazine, "That we won't need that splint after all."

"Would you sign it anyway?" the woman asked.

"No," Joe snapped, unaccountably furious.

Emily frowned at him and gave her head a gentle shake to the woman. "I'm sorry. I really don't sign things. I haven't done anything notable."

The woman snorted. "Except marry Matt Shephard. Closest I'll ever get to him."

"Still… no. I have a horse I need to see to."

Joe followed her gaze to where both horses were now trotting docily back to where the grooms waited by the train.

"Is that your horse?" he asked, "or have we been playing a scene?"

"That is my horse," she said, "And you'll have to ask Mrs. Merryweather about any scenes. I just met her on the train. You're the one who knows her."

She turned back to Mrs. Merryweather. Joe followed. "They will make beautiful babies, ya know. I don't suppose you'd like to sell her…"

All he got for that was a glare.

He shrugged.

"Don't you dare ruin all my hard work," he heard behind him.

He turned to see Mrs. Merryweather back in both shoes, her hat on, and her eyes shooting daggers.

"I'm not even gonna ask you how you pulled off this little trick," he said. "But I guess I want my money back."

"You don't want Graymist?" she demanded, hands on hips. "A prince among horses? What is the matter with you?"

"I'll take him," Mrs. Shephard said.

He glared, feeling as if the rug had been pulled out from under him. "I don't like practical jokes."

"Neither do I," Mrs. Merryweather insisted, stepping right up to him. "Well… all right, I do. But this isn't one of them. Graymist is yours, no matter what you decide today. He has made his decision and I won't turn my back on him. But don't turn down the opportunity of a lifetime just because you think you're not worthy of Emily over here." Suddenly she chuckled, an ancient female sound.

"Truth is, no man is worth any woman. But that's a secret we like to keep quiet or else there'd be no more babies. You want babies, don't you?"

Now Mrs. Shephard was staring at both of them like they'd lost their minds. He wasn't all that sure she wasn't right. "You mean with me?" she demanded of the little woman. "That train left the station a long time ago."

"It was Matt who couldn't have the babies, Emily," the woman gently said. "Not you. Trust me."

Now Emily stood there with her mouth open, frozen like a statue. "Don't... do that," she ground out, and suddenly Joe wanted to hold her. Just that, hold her until that terrible pain left her eyes.

But Mrs. Merryweather was there before him. "Dear girl," she said, hand on arm. "I never lie about such things. I don't joke. If you and Joe here take a chance... a mighty chance, I'll admit it, but what do you have to lose, really? You two will begin two great dynasties out on that ranch. You just have to believe it's possible."

"And what about me?" Joe asked, feeling less certain by the minute. "Don't I have something to say about these dynasties? You're making an awful lot of assumptions, old woman. I had money for a horse, not a dynasty, much less two."

"Well, isn't that convenient?" Mrs. Merryweather chirped, her eyes glittering, "Because at the end of six weeks, Emily will. And you'll be man enough to use that money to make your ranch into a haven for both of you. I know. It's how I've planned it forever."

"So, you mean to tell me," Emily said, "that you're going to make us fall in love and have babies and a horse empire?"

Again, Mrs. Merryweather giggled. "Oh dear me, no. I have no jurisdiction over the human heart."

"Then what have you been doing?"

"Putting everything in place to allow two hearts to find each other. Emily, you've paid enough penance for your marriage. You've wanted to return to the mountains since that day you left. Joe, you've been alone since your pa died on your twelfth birthday. You haven't even been able to call your own ranch home. You can have each other, and you can make a new home. What's wrong with that?"

And by damn if Joe couldn't think of a single thing.

He looked over at Emily who had the look of fragile glass. Emily with her flame-bright hair and brisk competence. Her spring green eyes and gentle hands. Emily who seemed to think she couldn't have children. Could he live with that?

Hell, until now he'd never thought he'd live with anyone. As hard as he'd worked just to get this far, he'd never had enough extra imagination for it. Could he take the risk of inviting this woman into his life?

Could he take the risk not to?

He decided he'd thought about it long enough. Walking right up to her, he pulled her up off the ground, surprised somehow that she was of a height to tuck right against his shoulder, and he cupped her face in his calloused hands. And he kissed her. He kissed her with everything in him, all his longing and loneliness and hunger. All his dreams that, until this moment, had seemed to be wasted. And when he finally pulled back, he realized that he hadn't been the only one storing up all those needs.

He looked down into those suddenly clangorous eyes. He wrapped his arms around her, thinking how perfectly she fit. "What do you think?"

Emily looked up into his eyes. He saw tears swelling in hers, and suddenly realized that he couldn't bear it if she turned away.

"Please."

She lifted a smooth hand to his cheek. "We could try."

He nodded. "That's all we can ask. Time to get those horses settled now, isn't it?"

"Is all this real?" Emily finally asked the old woman before she followed him away.

"Of course it is," the little lady huffed.

"And you're my fairy godmother."

She got another bright, tinkling laugh. "Oh, no dear," she said, patting Joe's arm. "I'm his."

* * *

Six weeks later, Emily left Reno on the same train heading the other way. Six weeks after that, she and Joe were married in a little Methodist chapel in Jackson. And against all odds, they did found two dynasties, one human, one equine. They named their first foal Misty Gray, and their first daughter Merry. And they really did live happily after.

9

LOVE AND THE LONELY

Mathew Kaufman

"I'm here. I love you. I don't care if you need to stay up crying all night long, I will stay with you. There's nothing you can ever do to lose my love. I will protect you until you die, and after your death I will still protect you. I am stronger than depression and I am braver than loneliness and nothing will ever exhaust me."
– Elizabeth Gilbert (Eat, Pray, Love)

Chapter One

Cal twisted the throttle on his Harley. The engine thundered into action, propelling him forward. Trees lined both sides of the road and whipped by in a blur as the bike sped by. He smiled. It had been a long time since he had gotten out of Vegas.

It was nice to leave the city behind. Just the thought of the city's constantly blinding lights disgusted him. The smells; the sounds; the grime. Gone. Replaced by nature. Deep reds, greens, and a myriad of other colors replaced the brown, brown, and brown of the desert.

"Yap! Yap!" his dog Scooter barked. Cal looked at the sidecar, one he'd had specifically made for Scooter after he'd adopted him. The pup's ears whipped back in the wind. His eyes tracked a squirrel as it jumped tree to tree. "Yap! Yap!" Cal reached over and rubbed Scooter's head. The dog panted with excitement and content.

They had been inseparable since Cal returned from Iraq. He had been in a real bad place. The darkest. But then, one day, Cal was walking to the corner store to get some beer and there he was in all his mangy glory. Scooter. Every rib was visible. He swore that he saw the dogs heart beat through its emaciated body.

Cal chuckled quietly to himself as he recalled the forty minutes it took to catch that damn dog. The little shit had him running between dumpsters, jumping through bushes, and crawling under just about everything a chihuahua could get under. Everything!

He finally caught him and when he lifted the pup into the air, the dog bit him. First on the hand, then on the nose. He remembered the flash of anger that ripped through him. He had just wanted to take him home and feed him. Ungrateful little shit.

Once the "vicious mauling" stopped, Cal held him one handed while removing his belt. He slid it around the dog's neck in a makeshift leash. They finished the walk to the store where Cal bought some Budweiser and dog food. They had been together ever since. And that was two years ago.

Cal returned his attention back to the road ahead. He accelerated through the next corner.

"Almost there, Scoot!" he said.

"Yip! Yip!"

"You excited? Me too!"

As he turned the next corner, the sun broke through the treetops, casting a blinding white light in Cal's eyes. He hit the brakes. There was a corner coming. The wheels squealed under the force of the sudden stop. The motorcycle began to break traction and spin.

"Shit!"

He hit the gas and tried to straighten out the bike. It continued to spin, faster now. The white light pulsed in his eyes like a paparazzi's flash, each one blinding and disorienting him further. More screeching. A lone bark escaped the blur that was Scooter.

Cal couldn't see his buddy, or anything else but white for that matter. His mind raced as he leaned left and right and worked the controls. With a jolt, the bike came to a sudden stop. Scooter yelped as he struck the wall of the sidecar. Cal flew over Scooter and crashed violently into a nearby pine tree. He felt the lights go out as his eyes filled with blackness.

* * *

Cal awoke to the feeling on a sopping tongue slathering his face with slobber. *Scooter.*

"Alright, Jesus Christ… You trying to drown me too?"

His head pounded as he opened his eyes. The world was upside-down and that confused the hell out of him. It took him a minute to realize that he was laying on his head and shoulders with his feet in the air. Not something he cared for.

He rolled to one side, his legs crashed onto the ground. *That's better.* He surveyed the surroundings and saw that during the spin, one of the tires had caught traction in the dirt and it came into the curve and well… ouch.

He removed his helmet and checked himself for injuries. *Nothing. That could have been worse.*

"How you doing, Scoot? he asked the dog, as if expecting an answer. The dog lay beside him panting nervously. Cal ran his hands over his little buddy checking him for injuries. Scooter didn't make a peep.

"Looks like we are A-Okay, buddy. We got damn lucky. Let's get the hell outta here," he said and picked up Scooter. Cal checked out the bike before placing the dog back in the sidecar. He grabbed his helmet off the ground and tried to pull it on.

A jolt of pain ripped through his right hand. Before he even saw it, wetness ran across his fingers. *Blood.* He lowered the helmet and saw, right on top, was a six-inch crushed section of fiberglass. Sharp pieces jutted outward throughout the scar.

He dropped the helmet to the ground and explored his new wound. It wasn't as bad as it felt. Across his index finger was a quarter-inch laceration. It was nothing a little tape, glue, or whatever couldn't fix. His commander would have said, "Rub some dirt on it and stop being a pussy, for fucks sake." He would have been right too… If he wasn't dead. Another casualty of war. One that no amount of dirt-rubbing will fix.

Enough of that shit. Cal wiped the blood on his pants and climbed back onto his bike. With a flick of the started, the engine roared to life and once again, they were off.

135

Chapter Two

"The loneliest moment in someone's life is when they are watching their whole world fall apart, and all they can do is stare blankly."
—F. Scott Fitzgerald

"Come on Scooter. You ready to get this shit set up?" The dog sprang out of the side car and ran around to Cal. Together, they grabbed the tent bag and set out in separate directions. "This way, dude."

"Grrr"

"Come on, Scooter, over here."

"Rrrrr. Rrrrr. Grrrrrr," he growled, tugging at the tent bag.

"Ok... Looks like we're going over there." He followed the chihuahua a few feet down the hill. Scooter growled once more and let go before unleashing a torrent of urine, marking this as his spot! "Alright... But I'm not sleeping next to your pee," Cal said, rolling his eyes before getting to work on the tent.

In no time, despite Scooter's best efforts, the tent and hammock were erected, they had a circle of rocks for a firepit and were now off collecting sticks.

"Shouldn't be long 'til they get here, bud." The dog bolted into a nearby pile of brush. "Looks like I'm talking to myself. Sounds about right. Guess I can take a little nap until they get here."

Cal sighed. *They should be here by now. I wonder where they could be?* He figured that he would hear their motorcycles rumbling up the road if he did fall asleep. And even if he didn't, they would wake him up when they arrived.

He retrieved his cowboy hat from behind the seat in his sidecar. It was a tattered, well-worn thing. The brim was stained dark with oil badly in need of a change. His dad gave him that hat. His first cowboy hat. He remembered the day he got it like it was yesterday.

* * *

His family gathered around the living room celebrating his twenty-first birthday. His dad handed him a box while wearing a grin so big it could be seen from space.

"'Bout time you had one of these, boy. No self-respecting man should live in the west without one," his dad said. He took the box–a big 'ol cube–from his dad's hands. He was shocked at how light it was. What could a box this big have in it that would weigh so little?

Curiosity tore through him like a wildfire through the mountains of California. He shredded the wrapping paper, furiously searching for clues on each sliver of box he exposed. Eventually, the word Resistol appeared.

"No way, dad! Really?" He ripped the lid off the box and there is was, a George Strait Silver Eagle Special. He shook with excitement, like that of a child seeing Santa Clause for the first time.

"Dad, this is too much. It's so expensive."

"Nonsense. You deserve it. You're a good kid..." He paused. "No. You're a good man. You did us proud. You're serving your country and taking freedom to people who have only dreamed about it. I love you, son."

He stood and pulled his dad in, giving him a hug. "I love you too, dad. I wish mom could be here."

"Me too, kid. Me too."

The embrace lasted a few more seconds before they parted, returning to their seats. Neither spoke again for several minutes.

His dad passed three weeks later from the cancer he'd never told anyone he had. He had left a letter behind that said he didn't want to burden anyone with the stress of watching him die slowly. He didn't want his family to worry. He wanted them to remember him for the man he was, not the disease he had.

* * *

Cal sat, sinking into the hammock, and laid back. He put the hat over his face and fell asleep.

Chapter Three

"Never confuse a single defeat with a final defeat."
—F. Scott Fitzgerald

Sleep had a firm grip on Cal. His mind wandered into a dreamy state. His wife, Beth, was there. He was there. It was Sunday morning. They were doing what they did every Sunday morning–

making breakfast together.

Clad only in their underwear they moved around each other like ballet dancers. He stirred the pancake batter, she the eggs. They kissed and nibbled each other's necks playfully. He kissed her neck and nibbled her nose.

Cal watched as her smile spread widely across her face. That was the smile he fell in love with. Like the rest of her, it was perfection. She rinsed the bowl from the counter, wetted her hands and splashed him, soaking his T-shirt. His pecs, topped with mocha brown nipples, peeked through.

She pulled him into her body, licking and sucking on his neck. Saliva glimmered in the morning light as it shown through the window. She ran her fingers lightly down his covered chest, stopping at his navel, circling it gently. He loved this. His navel had always been a sensitive point of arousal for him. Today was no different.

He heard his breathing deepen as she lifted the tee up, exposing his abs, and eventually tugged it over his head. Once again, she traced her way down to his navel, this time with her tongue. It left behind a slick line of moisture which she blew on lightly.

He felt his penis engorging, yearning for her touch. He felt her breasts press into his thighs as she knelt in front of him. She kissed lower and tugged lightly on his boxers. He was now fully erect and throbbing at her every touch, but she obviously wasn't done teasing him. She kissed the now exposed V of his hardened body. He tossed his head back and moaned at her touch.

She pecked at his erection through the fabric. He looked down and saw that his member was drooling with excitement. She licked the wetness, tasting his love potion. She pulled harder on the cloth. He was clean cut above his member, and his short hairs came into view.

He watched as she pulled harder on his underwear. Each second, more of his manhood came into view. She reached in, grasping it with her hand; it was warm as it touched his skin. She exposed him completely. The veins atop the shaft pounded with excitement. He could feel her breath on him.

He wanted her, needed her. He breathed in sharply as she took him into her mouth…

* * *

Cal startled awake to his dog's barking. He tried to jump to his feet, not remembering he was in a hammock, and failed to gain his balance before slamming face-first into the dirt. His head spun.

"Scooter! Where are you?" he yelled as he regained his footing. The growling grew louder in the bushes. The sun had set, and he couldn't see where any movement was coming from, but it grew louder with each passing second.

Suddenly, Scooter bolted out of the weeds, jumping with excitement. He lunged at Cal who caught him like a fur missile.

"What is it, bud? Why the hell are you so happy?"

Scooter panted wildly; strings of drool dangled from his jowls. He looked up at the continued rustling. That's when he saw her. Beth.

"How…"

"Shh. I'll explain everything, I promise. But we have to go right now," Beth said.

"Why?"

"I don't have time to explain. You must trust me. We have to go."

"I missed you so much. But how are you here? You died in a plane crash."

"Shh. Not now. Soon, but not now."

Without another word, she grabbed his hand and yanked him into the woods, almost making him fall. He realized that Scooter was still in his arms and despite being a chihuahua, was getting heavy.

They ran for what seemed like forever. "How far are we gonna go here? When the hell are you gonna tell me what's going on?" Finally, they slowed to a walk and eventually stopped.

"Okay. We are far enough for now. Out of its immediate range."

"Out of what's range?"

"I missed you, Cal. I missed everything about you. Your smell, your taste, your face. I've been watching you from… I'm just going to call it Heaven. It is the easiest way to explain it. I couldn't watch you anymore, though. They caught me."

"Who? Caught you doing what?"

"Stop asking questions for a minute, Cal. I'll explain. So you see, if you die, you go to this place where you wait to be reborn. Your needs are satisfied there. Food, entertainment, everything. But you are not allowed to see the people that are still alive.

"Well, I found out a way. There are gods… Many different ones. Not all of them are good. Some of them will do all they can to make you happy. Some of them will do just the opposite. When you arrive, you are assigned to a god for the duration of your stay.

"Mine was a bastard god named Somnus. He hid us away from the others. Made us his slaves. We built towers in his image. Great thrones for him to sit upon and rule. One day, while servicing his chambers I came across a viewing portal to this world. It was tuned to *you*. I couldn't believe it. Why would he be watching you?

"Over the next few days I watched as he killed your mom, then your dad. He was purposefully killing everyone you loved."

"Holy shit! Why?" Cal asked.

"I wondered the same thing. So, one night I snuck in his room and hid under his bed. I was terrified, but I had to know."

"Jesus, Beth."

"That evening he returned to his bedroom and began using the viewer. He was watching you on your ride up here. I saw you and Scooter, who is adorable by the way. Then I saw him reach into the viewer and cause your accident. All it took was a simple swirl of his finger."

She paused. A tear rolled down her cheek.

"What is it?" he asked.

"I saw you and Scooter–" Tears now flowed like rivers over her cheeks. "I saw you die."

"No way. I'm fine. I'm right here. Look at me. Beth, I promise, I'm fine."

"I'm sorry, Cal. You and Scooter died. If you don't believe me, look over there," she said pointing toward brush atop a nearby hill.

Cal jumped to his feet, eager to prove her wrong. He ran up the hill, pushing twigs and other brush out of his way. Scooter followed closely behind with his floppy little tongue swaying about. A few seconds later, they crested the hill.

He didn't see anything. "What are you talking about? There's nothing here."

She stepped up next to him. "Right there," she said and pointed down the steep embankment.

He saw it. "I don't believe it. That can't be us."

"It is, baby. I'm so sorry," Beth sobbed. "I'm so sorry."

Cal stepped down the hill toward his wrecked motorcycle. As he got closer he saw his flannel shirt, the one he was wearing when it happened. He saw a pale white hand atop the sidecar. It was holding on to a brown clump of fur. Scooter.

"I don't want to see any more," he said, turning around.

"You don't have to, baby. I just wanted you to know I was telling the truth."

"What the hell do I do now? A few minutes ago I was alive and well, now... Not so much."

"Somnus is here, on Earth. He has been looking for you since the accident. There is a window of time where he can't see you after you die. That window has passed, and you are now visible to him again and so am I."

"I assume you have a plan?" he asked.

"My plan was pretty short sighted. I just wanted to see you again."

"Well, here I am," Cale said, wide-eyed. "Now let's not die—or whatever. Do you know how to get back to where you came from?"

"Yes. When you come through, there is a 'window' back to the other side. It will remain where you came through it. Mine is a few hundred yards that way," she said, pointing west.

"Shall we?" he asked.

"I'll do whatever I have to to stay with you," she said. "I can't lose you again."

The two started running toward the window. Cal tripped, and Scooter went flying. He yipped as flew out of sight.

"Scooter!" Cal yelled.

He heard the dog from somewhere in front of him yip in pain. Both Beth and he rushed toward the noise. As they broke through the brush into a clearing, there stood Somnus, holding the limp body of Scooter.

"Lose something?" he said, dropping Scooter to the ground.

Somnus was dressed in long black robes that flowed freely around him and obscured everything behind him. His face wasn't visible from where they stood but his eyes... They glowed like neon. A pair of deep red dots, they flooded his hood with light.

"Who are you?" Cal asked.

"You know who I am. Don't play me for a fool. I know she told you all about me. Now I'm here to take my property home. Don't you want to see your mommy and daddy again, Cal? They are in my service. My slaves. I'll let you see them. Once."

"Why me?" he asked. "Why did you kill my family?"

"Because I need workers. I need slaves to build my kingdom. I don't have time to do it myself. It's far easier to take what I need from this place. Your puny little lives are meaningless. You are like ants, scurrying around, burning up this world, using all its resources. You're nothing but blood sucking leeches."

"We may be leeches, but who the hell are you to decide we don't deserve to live?"

"I'm your god, boy. Don't test my patience."

"What if we don't want to serve you anymore?" Beth asked.

"Then you will die."

"So be it, then. I'm not living under the reign of a tyrant like you," she said.

"Me either," Cal said. He saw Scooter move and whistled for the dog. Scooter limped to him. "Let's get this over with."

"Very well. I'm going to make your parents suffer for your choice," Somnus said.

Cal turned to Beth, "I love you, and I'll always love you." He bent down and picked up Scooter. "I love you too, buddy." He kissed Beth and his tummy tingled like it was the first time. Scooter licked both their faces.

The three of them exchanged their last kisses. Cal watched as Somnus opened his robe and drew out a glowing sword. He knew this was the end. Somnus raised the sword and swung. Cal pulled Beth and Scooter in tight.

The blade made a horrific hum as it whizzed through the air.

"ENOUGH!" a voice thundered.

Cal opened his eyes in time to see Somnus fly across the landscape before crashing into a tree with enough force it snapped in half.

"No..." Somnus sputtered.

"You have gone too far, Somnus. You have overstepped and taken the lives of happy, healthy humans. You have killed when you should have coddled. You have stolen from me my viewer. A device meant to help humans. To give them a nudge in the right direction— and you have used it for murder."

"I can explain—"

"There is nothing to explain, Somnus. I found your realm, filled with statues devoted to yourself. Your conduct warrants banishment to the nether, a realm where you shall spend eternity alone. One where you can no longer have influence over anyone."

Somnus opened his mouth to speak, but, with the blink of an eye, vanished.

"Now, what am I to do with you three?" the voice boomed.

"Who are you?" Cal asked.

A white light illuminated the area in front of Cal. A figure dressed in white with a flowing white cloak appeared.

"I am Astrild, Goddess of Love. I was alerted to the goings on here when your mate, Beth, crossed worlds to find you. Her act of love drew my attention. I saw your suffering. How you loved her. How you loved your big rat."

"Um, it's a dog, and his name is Scooter," Cal said.

"Not the point, human. What to do with you from here is the problem."

"What are our choices?" Beth asked.

"Stay dead and reunite with your family and live forever in my ethereal plane, or I could restore your lives and send you back to Earth. I will restore your family as well, but I will not be able to provide for you, look out for you, or care for you. Should you die, you die. I'll give the choice to you."

Cal looked at Beth and Scooter. "What would you like to do?" Cal asked Beth.

"Will you bring Scooter back to life also?" Beth asked. "He has taken very good care of Cal, and I know he loves him."

"Yes, yes, of course. On that note, I will do even better. Because you showed such affection toward the rat, I'll let him live as long as Cal does. But you must choose now."

"Cal?" she asked.

"I think you know," he said. "Scooter?"

"Yip! Yip!"

"You heard the rat," Cal said.

The world flashed white...

Chapter Four

"Live to the point of tears."
— Albert Camus

Cal woke up in his bed, wearing Scooter like a hat on his pillow. He smelled bacon and heard someone downstairs. Could it really be?

He leapt from the bed and thundered downstairs. He followed the smell to the kitchen where he saw her...

"Beth!" he yelled. He ran to her as fast as his legs would carry him. He embraced and kissed her feverishly, twirling her around the kitchen. "I love you so much!"

"I love you too, babe!" she said. "Look at what Astrild did for us."

She walked him to the back door. His jaw slackened as he saw the pastures, the horses, the bales of hay. Scooter rumbled down the stairs behind him. Cal turned to scoop him up. In his mouth was the hat his father had given him. He pulled it out of Scooter's mouth and looked inside it.

A piece of paper was stuck on the felt inside. Cal set his pup down and pulled the paper out. It read:

Cal,

You have your wish. You are back on Earth with your love and your rat dog. I found your hat and motorcycle. They are both in your "garage." I doubt you'll be using it as much as you used to. Enjoy your life on earth and take care not to let death befall you. I took some liberties and set you up for a good life here. I hope you enjoy the place called Reno.

Astrild

The note flickered and disappeared. Cal scooped up Scooter again. "Thanks, buddy," he said.

"Yip! Yip! Yip!"

Cal looked at Beth and grasped her hand. Their life started for the second time that day. They knew what they had. Love.

"Death must be so beautiful. To lie in the soft brown earth, with the grasses waving above one's head, and listen to silence. To have no yesterday, and no to-morrow. To forget time, to forget life, to be at peace."
—Oscar Wilde, The Canterville Ghost

10

ONE NIGHT

Elle J. Rossi

Hannah Armstrong stood on the neighbor's sagging porch, bare toes digging into a "Welcome" mat that should have been tossed a decade ago, fingers curled and poised to knock.

This was stupid. Sighing, she let her arm fall and waged the same internal debate she'd had going on for the last twenty-four hours.

No way would he agree to it.

But… he owed her.

Sort of. If one could consider a favor more than ten years old to still be an outstanding debt.

Yes. He owed her.

The favor had cost her more than she would ever admit. Not even to her therapist. If she had one. Which she didn't, and never would. Who needed a professional when she could spar with the voices in her head and save about a bazillion dollars?

She'd just have to find another way, even if something about this way appealed to her more than she cared to analyze. Beating her head against the wall seemed like an even better idea, until she realized she was actually doing it. The screen door knocked hard against the frame.

Shit.

Hannah whirled and tore down the steps, dropping a stream of cuss words that would make a preacher drop to his knees and pray for her soul, when her dress snagged on the railing and slowed her

145

escape. The screen door cried louder than a pair of fighting cats, and she knew she'd been busted. Really, did he ever plan to fix this broken house? Cringing, she turned and offered up an innocent smile.

No words. Just one honeyed brow arched in question.

Leaning against the railing, she discreetly tried to free her dress from the clutches of a nail. "I need to borrow your truck."

Brody West, the man Hannah had *very* mistakenly told once—a *very* long time ago, so it totally didn't count—that he was way too sexy to live, leaned against the doorjamb and bit into a shiny red apple with an audible crunch. He wiped away the juice with the back of his hand, and even that didn't knock off a single point from the sexy scale.

"You need to borrow my truck?"

He wasn't close enough to touch her, but his voice rumbled through the air and caressed her skin. She blamed the full-body shiver on the breeze and would argue with anyone who dared to challenge her that hot southerly winds could indeed be chilly. Which would also explain the state of her nipples. Though he didn't comment, she knew he'd noticed her reaction to his voice. Brody noticed everything. Note to self: Never leave home without a bra.

"Yes," she answered, her voice embarrassingly breathless. She cleared her throat and prayed the next words that came out of her mouth sounded a lot less like Marilyn Monroe.

"My brand new, has less than fifty miles, and zero dents on it truck?"

"Do you have another one?" She commanded her eyes to stay locked on his, but the bitches went straight-up traitor and perused Brody up and down as if they were trying to pick a suspect from a line-up. He wore his grey T-shirt just snug enough to hint at the lean muscle beneath. The Mason Fire Department logo drew her gaze to his right pec, which may or may not have twitched under her scrutiny. A pair of well-worn jeans covered equally-muscled legs. Legs she did not gawk at when he'd gone for a run earlier this morning. And late last night. And yesterday morning. Always, always plead innocent. No matter what. When she finally managed to look at his face again, she saw amusement and a whole lot of heat in his blue eyes.

Nope. Not going there. This man was as far off limits as one could get.

Though, at the moment, she couldn't quite remember why. "Soooo? Where are the keys?"

Brody took a step and let the screen door slam behind him. "The keys?"

"Yes. The keeeeys," she said slowly. "What's wrong with you? Did you eat a parrot for breakfast?" She pulled on her dress but the fabric wouldn't budge.

He closed the distance, his steps as sure and determined as a top-notch predator, and Hannah sucked in a breath. "You know what?" she said, wrenching her dress free. She'd cry about the tear later. "Forget I even asked." He blocked her retreat with an arm on each side of her body. Damn, this man had a presence. He still hadn't touched her, not that she wanted him to, but the temperature change in the air could have blown the top off a thermometer.

"What's wrong with your car, Hannah?"

She shook her head. "Nothing, why?"

"I'm just curious as to why you need to borrow my brand-new truck."

Her turn to arch a brow, though she doubted it had quite the same effect. "And I'm curious as to why you need to breathe all over me." She shoved him with both hands. He didn't budge. "Back up."

Brody quirked a grin and stepped back. "I was saving your life, and you, Miss Temperamental, don't sound very appreciative."

"I didn't realize I was in danger."

He held up a rusty nail.

"Wow." She rolled her eyes. "You're a real hero."

His gaze raked over her body in a very rogue-like fashion. "You looking for a hero, Armstrong?"

Nope. Under no circumstances did she need a hero who had *saved* just about every female under the age of forty-five within a hundred-mile radius. Oh, yes. Now she remembered why she'd stuck him in the no-way-in-hell zone. Brody brought the phrase "man-ho" to a whole new level. Not to mention the other big reason she would never give in to lust and curiosity and sleep with him. "Definitely not." She lifted her chin. "I need a truck and I see I'll just have to get one somewhere else."

His hot gaze seemed to grow just a bit hotter and there was nothing flirtatious about it. "I'll drive. Where are we going?"

What? No. "You can't go, Brody." Just thinking about tonight had her nerves rattled. The last thing she needed was to have Brody distracting her from her job. Well, potential job. If everything went as planned. The fact that ghosts were involved might send shivers down her spine (not the good kind), but she was going to don her big-girl panties and make it through the night. The whole night.

"Why not? Just point me to what you need loaded and I'll help you. Even though you weren't willing to help me the other night."

Right. She'd all but slammed the door in his face when he'd come over to ask if she'd had any oatmeal. Seriously? Oatmeal? It wouldn't have mattered what he'd asked for. His timing had been bad.

"I will be the bigger person here," he continued, his voice a mixture of smoke and gravel.

No doubt about that. Everything about Brody was bigger. She swallowed hard as butterflies swarmed in her belly. How had she ever thought this would be a good idea? "Thanks, but never mind. I'll figure something out."

She made it down the steps and, *halleluiah*, she was in the clear. She could just take her car and camp out in that the whole night, but it was about the size of a loaf of bread. Surely that made it an easy target for specters. Documenting supernatural activity was one thing. Being possessed by a ghost was quite another.

"Is Jake coming to help anytime soon?"

Hannah jerked to a stop but didn't turn. "He's not coming at all."

"You've got to be shitting me? He's leaving all of this to you to take care of?"

She shrugged, a gesture that belied how she truly felt. "It's no big deal. Jake is dealing with some stuff right now."

Brody moved in front of her, tossed the apple core into the yard. "He's my best friend, Hannah. I know exactly what he's dealing with. And none of that excuses him from this."

Staring past him, she said, "He's my brother. *I've* excused him from this."

He reached out and cupped her chin. She didn't dare look at him. If she did, she'd crumble into his arms. "Let me help you."

Hannah shook her head. "I don't need help." She just needed to breathe.

"But you need to borrow my truck."

She nodded once.

"Fine," he said with a cocky grin that roused more than a little suspicion.

Her gaze jerked back to his. "Fine? I can use your truck?"

"Answer one question for me and I'll get you the keys."

Hope bloomed and spread through her chest, but she squelched it and narrowed her eyes. She'd played these games with Brody before and she'd lost every single time. "No way."

* * *

Brody barked out a laugh. "Why, Hannah Caroline Armstrong, I've never known you to be scared of anything." He wet his lips and waited for the challenge to show in her chocolate brown eyes. Ah, yes. There it was. He'd take that any day over the grief she'd tried to hide.

She lifted her chin. Long, dark hair blew across her face and for a moment he was dumbstruck by her beauty. Yeah, he'd noticed before. Shit, a blind man couldn't miss her, but there were moments when this woman stirred his blood and made him wish for things that could never be. Her choice. Not his.

She shoved her hair back and leveled him with a pointed look. "I'm not scared of you."

"Prove it," he said, sliding his hand over her elbow and guiding her back across the yard toward her mother's house. Damn, she had soft skin. He took a chance and caressed the inside of her arm with his thumb.

She snatched her arm away as if a rattler had taken hold. "Fine. What do you want to know?"

So much, but if he knew one thing, he knew Hannah, and digging in would get him nowhere. "How long will you be in town?"

He watched her wrestle with the question, doing what she always did, which would be to answer with the least amount of commitment.

Hannah stopped, tilted her head. "That's a tough one."

Weren't they all? "Not really. You must have some sort of a plan?"

She smiled and the wattage nearly undid him. "Come on, Brody. You know better than that. I don't do plans."

"But you're here."

149

The smile faded. "I'm here doing what needs to be done."

"Alone."

"Yes. Alone." Her expression hardened into the mask she so often wore. "I'm good alone."

"Yeah," he agreed, though he couldn't say he was happy about it. "You always have been."

Head high now, she said, "I've answered your question, and therefore you must hand over the keys. But..."

"But?" This should be good.

She smoothed her hands over her dress. "Well, I've decided to be honorable and let you know why I need your truck."

"Honorable. That's not new for you. Me, on the other hand..."

"Yeah, yeah. The entire state knows about your honor status— or lack thereof."

"You're exaggerating."

"Not even a little."

Did this mean she was interested in his status? "Maybe a couple counties. Definitely not the state, but a man can have goals."

Hannah snorted. "Anyway."

Brody laughed at her lame attempt to change the subject. He decided to go easy on her. For now. "You were about to tell me why you need Big Black."

Another snort. "You named your truck. How old are you again?"

"You know exactly how old I am. Stop stalling, Armstrong."

"Come on," she said, turning. "I need to show you something."

And damn if all kinds of *somethings* didn't drift through his mind in brilliant detail. He stared after her as she walked away, her long dress flowing around her ankles. His gaze locked on her bare feet, the charm from her ankle bracelet hanging low, and a surge of blood went straight to his groin. Feminine with a dash of tomboy. Could a combination be any more erotic? He'd never been a foot man, so to speak, but he was willing to give it a try. Perhaps because Hannah was unattainable, a challenge that should be left alone was what intrigued him most. Maybe that's why the idea of her writhing under him, screaming his name, held so much appeal he'd had a hard time sleeping since she'd come back to town. Two words: Vivid dreams.

"You coming?"

Nearly. He met her eyes and flashed her the smile that had a one hundred percent panty dropping success rate. "You hinting at something there?"

She shook her head. "Feel free to tell your brain to leave the gutter."

He smiled again. Got nada in return. There you had it. Hannah wasn't like any other woman. Laughing, Brody followed her down the driveway, past the porch to the back of the house. She disappeared around the side of the garage. When he caught up, he came to an abrupt stop.

"What the hell is that?" He scrubbed his hand over his face, but the thing didn't disappear.

She snapped her head toward him. "What do you mean, what is it? It's clearly a camper."

"Nope." He shook his head slowly, back and forth. "You absolutely cannot use the word clearly here. That," he pointed, "is not a camper."

"Why not?"

"For one thing, it's too small to be a camper. But more importantly, it looks like a rainbow threw up on it. No sane person would allow you in their campground with *that*."

"Ha ha. Funny as that may be, it's the perfect size for me and there isn't a rainbow color on there. Those are jewel tones."

Brody had a hankering to make sure his jewels were still intact. Just looking at this *camper* was enough to make the boys shrivel. The damned thing looked like a patchwork quilt his Grandmother had made. The same one he'd promptly shoved in a closet. "This is what you need my truck for," he said, shaking his head again. "Big Black towing Rainbow Brite."

"Yes?"

He turned his gaze on her and got a kick out of watching her squirm. "And just where will you be going?"

"Yeah… about that. Do you want a beer?"

* * *

Hannah couldn't believe it. Not only had Brody agreed to let her borrow his truck, he'd offered to *go* with her. And for the record, the only reason she was excited about that was because she was scared out of her mind. It definitely had nothing to do with the fact that she'd be spending an entire night in very close quarters with a sexy fireman. Specifically, this sexy fireman.

No, the fear came from spending the night in the middle of the desert. The *haunted* desert to be more precise. She'd heard stories about this place since she was a kid. In high school, some of her friends had camped out here. Half of them had come back scared out of their minds, while others called it lame.

"So," Brody said, leaning against his truck. "Explain to me again why you're doing this?"

She blew out a breath, took in the expanse of desert surrounding her before angling her body toward his. She smiled. "You afraid?"

"Not even a little. You?"

To lie or not to lie? "Terrified."

"Then why did you agree to do it?"

"If I don't do it, I don't get the job." She'd recently been offered a job with an online magazine to travel the country and write articles about her experiences. The gig would take her to strange places. She'd only stay one night, write about the adventure, and if it was good enough, they'd publish it and she'd get paid. Hannah had no doubt her stories would be good enough. She was a strong writer. And usually she didn't mind being alone, but there was something about this first assignment that had her on edge. She didn't believe in ghosts, per se. But she didn't *not* believe in them either. Add to the fact that she'd been dealing with the ghosts of her childhood since her mother had passed a few weeks ago, and her typically cool and calm self had transformed into someone she didn't recognize.

"This job that important to you?"

Yes and no. She'd never been content in one place very long, so the travel aspect spoke to her. Yet the idea of being told where to go next without having any say in the decision making process kind of ate at her. "Maybe," she answered with a shrug. "I'm gonna give it one night and see."

Brody's lips curled into a half-smile.

Hannah narrowed her eyes. "What?"

"One night, huh? Sounds like a challenge."

She had no idea where he was going with that. "Day by day, I guess."

"And say you like this gig. Then what? You and Rainbow Brite hit the open road?"

She shrugged. "Well, not tomorrow, if that's what you mean. I still have to pack up the rest of Mom's… things." She struggled with what to call her mother's possessions.

"I can help."

Hannah shook her head, tucked her hands into her pockets. It might have been sweltering hot during the day, but as the sun dipped below the horizon, the temperature dipped along with it. "I appreciate that, but I've got it." There was no way she could let him inside that house. Guilt swamped her. She should have come home more often. Maybe she could have done something before… Before what? Her mother had started hoarding things the moment Hannah's father had left. Hannah had been fourteen then. Within a year, it had gotten so bad, she'd stopped inviting friends over. She and Jake had gone to Brody's house as often as they could. Anything to take a break from the constant chaos and claustrophobia.

"Would you still have done this if I hadn't been able to come?"

"Whoa, wait a minute." She stabbed his chest with her finger. "You invited yourself, remember? I didn't need you; I only needed your truck." That didn't mean she wasn't glad he'd offered to tag along. Although she suspected his reason was more to protect Big Black than little Hannah Armstrong.

He wrapped his fingers around hers. "I'm off for the next seventy-two hours, and I'm always up for an adventure."

"Of the sexual gymnastics kind," she muttered to herself, pulling from his grasp.

Brody chuckled and she felt the sexy rumble all the way to her toes.

"You know, this is the second time you mentioned my sex life today. Interested?"

She snorted. "In you? Hardly." Yeah, like so hard. But she wouldn't tell him.

He reached over and slid his hand around her nape, gently massaging her tight muscles. "I'm gonna call bullshit on that."

She forced herself to shrug away from his touch when all she really wanted to do was close her eyes and lean into it. "Call it whatever you want. You're not all that." She nearly laughed at her own lie. Brody West *was* all that and not just because of his looks. If you could see past his sexual conquests, he really was rather perfect. She was tempted to give in, to see if he was everything she'd dreamed him to be.

And why the hell shouldn't she? She was a grown woman and if she wanted to have a one-night stand she could do it. Except could she really call it a one-night stand when she'd known this man her entire life?

"Might want to stop thinking so much. I see smoke and I'm off duty, remember?"

Hannah shook her head at him. "Right. You're off duty and I'm on. I'm not even sure what it is I'm supposed to do here. Do you think we should make noise to attract the ghosts, or should we be really quiet?" They'd been waiting for more than an hour and she'd yet to detect anything. Some story that would make.

"You're assuming ghosts exist."

"For tonight, I am. I mean there must be some truth to all the stories told about this place."

"Or one person made up a story and that story was told over and over again until it became a thing."

Shrugging, she said, "Well, I hope something happens tonight. I need something extraordinary to put on the page."

She turned to head into the camper, planning to grab a blanket, but Brody snagged her hand and pulled her to him.

Chest flush to his, she asked, "What are you doing?" She looked up and saw pure desire in his eyes.

He leaned close and she couldn't stop her tongue from wetting her lips.

"I'm giving you something extraordinary."

Before she could respond—though she had no idea what she would have said—Brody caught her bottom lip between his teeth. As if waiting for permission, he pulled back just enough to break contact. Hannah clenched her fists, desperately trying to fight a battle she'd already lost. With a combination of regret and relief, she looked up at him and nodded once. Brody groaned, crushed his mouth to hers and that was all it took for Hannah to lose herself. A thousand ghosts could have circled the camper in that moment and she wouldn't have noticed. Every breath, every moment, every fiber was wrapped up in Brody West. Why the hell had she waited so long to taste him?

Brody slid his hands down her arms, weaved his fingers through hers. Heat seared through her body. The feel of his tongue against hers had pure lust sparking fire in her veins.

Without breaking the kiss, he walked her backward until her back was flush against his truck. Hannah unlaced one of her hands from his and moved her fingertips over his shirt, making her way up to slide through his hair. Brody slowed the pace, bringing it to a level that was more passion than desperation. Somehow that got to her more. A soft gasp escaped, and she knew tonight was a game changer.

He pulled back and gazed down at her, heat evident in his gaze. "You okay?"

Thankfully, his breathing was every bit as ragged as hers. And she could have sworn he was shaking. Was he like that with all women? Jealousy stabbed her heart hard. "Not at all," she said, admitting to a truth probably better kept to herself.

"Me either. God, Hannah. That was—"

A blast of cold air swirled around them, stealing whatever Brody was about to say.

Hannah grabbed Brody's hand in a death grip, goose bumps dotting her skin. "Did you feel that?"

Brody turned, instantly becoming her shield. "Yeah. It's probably nothing. Probably just an air pocket."

She appreciated him trying to ease her fear, but his body, primed and on full alert, told her he didn't believe his own words.

"An air pocket that came to us?" She peeked around Brody and scanned the area. They must have been kissing for quite some time because the sun had slid so far down, the desert had turned to shades of twilight. The view would have been beautiful if she weren't so freaked out. "Now do you believe in ghosts?"

Brody looked over his shoulder. "I honestly don't know what I believe."

She could say the same. "Let's go inside for a bit." If there were ghosts out there, she needed to put a wall between them and her.

"Fine," he said, leading the way. "But you have to swear not to tell anyone I went glamping with you."

Hannah stopped—stopped moving, stopped breathing. "Do you have a girlfriend?"

Brody's gaze nearly bore a hole through her head. "Did you really just ask me that?"

Spine stiff, she said, "I did. You're the one who doesn't want anyone to know you're out here with me."

He blew out a long breath. "That's not what I said at all." He tugged her through the door, ducking to clear his head. "Sit down, Hannah."

She did, but only to put some distance between them.

He leaned against the counter, arms crossed over his broad chest. "I think we need to clear up a few things. Let's start with what you asked me. If I had a girlfriend, I wouldn't have kissed you."

She opened her mouth, but Brody barreled on.

"Contrary to what you think, I don't use women like that. Sure, I like to have fun, but only with one woman at a time, and not nearly as often as you seem to think."

Was it possible she'd let rumors spur on her imagination? She swallowed past the lump in her throat. "Sorry I jumped to conclusions."

Brody nodded. "Apology accepted. My comment earlier was a joke about your ball-shriveling camper, not about being with you."

"Oh."

He shoved away from the counter and crouched in front of her. "Yeah, *oh*. And here's another thing for your brain to process. I wouldn't have been with any other women these past years if you'd allowed me to be with you."

Her mind could not comprehend his words. What was he saying? "But..."

"But what?"

"How long have you felt this way?"

Brody smiled. "For as long as I can remember. Since my best friend's bratty little sister kept forcing her way into our fort."

"And prom?" That favor she'd done for him? He'd only asked her to be his date so he could pretend to go to the dance. But he and Jake had never had any intention of going. They'd gone to a party instead.

His brows bunched. "What about prom?"

"You asked me to the dance so I could cover for you and Jake. If you had been into me then, you would have taken me." She couldn't keep the hurt out of her voice. It still stung. The way she had been so giddy when he'd asked, only to quickly find out he hadn't wanted to take her at all.

"Damn, Hannah. I'm sorry. I didn't realize you wanted to go. You didn't seem that interested."

Apparently, her play-it-cool pep talk had worked too well. She hadn't wanted him to think she was some giddy girl.

"I was young and dumber than dumb. I wanted to take you. Trust me, I would rather have been there with you than hanging with a bunch of dudes getting stupid drunk. To be honest, I was a scared punk."

She stifled a laugh. "You? Scared? Sorry if I'm having a hard time wrapping my mind around that."

"I was scared to tell Jake I was into you. He'd been my best friend since kindergarten. He was so protective of you. I didn't want to screw that up."

Oh. She had nothing to say to that. He hadn't told her how he felt, but she hadn't told him either. Telling him he was sexy didn't count.

She traced his lips with her finger. Brody slid his palm up her thigh. His touch caused a powerful ache between her thighs.

"That's when everything changed between us. I wish you *had* said something, Hannah."

"Yeah, me too."

"By the time I got up the nerve to tell Jake I wanted to ask you out, you would hardly even look at me. Damn," he said with a sigh. "We wasted so much time."

Hannah chewed on her lip. "Maybe we can make up for it?"

Brody's hand snuck under the hem of her shirt, slowly making its way up until he palmed her breast. "I think we should give it our best shot."

She leaned into him, desperate for more, when a high-pitched wail tore through the walls of the camper. She launched herself into Brody's arms as the trailer swayed back and forth. A cabinet door flew open and a dish crashed against the counter. Her blood, heated by Brody's touch moments ago, turned to ice. The cold air they'd felt outside had nothing on this.

Brody urged her toward the bed. "It's okay. Wait here for a minute. I need to go outside."

"What? No!" She pulled her knees to her chest, making her body as small as she could. As if that would protect her from whatever demons were trying to kill them. Whatever was out there must have heard her thoughts, because the wail grew louder. She fought the urge to plug her ears and close her eyes.

"I won't be long. It's probably just the wind or some punk kids. Either way, I'm going to get you out of here."

She shook her head. "You can't go out there. Please, Brody. You can't leave me." Maybe she was being irrational, but she had a feeling if he stepped through that door she'd never see him again. Besides, the rocking had stopped, and the wail sounded more like wind than anything now. "Just come sit with me. We have to stay here."

Brody looked torn, but ultimately stretched out next to her. He brushed his fingers through her hair. "I wasn't going to leave you. I was going to rescue you. I was trying to protect you."

Hannah leaned into him. "You can't protect me if you're not with me."

He kissed her shoulder. "Is that what you want? For me to be with you?"

She knew what he was asking. She just wasn't sure if she was ready to answer. She stalled by kissing him. But Brody broke the kiss all too soon.

"You need to answer the question before we take this any further."

God, her heart was pounding. Was it from the ghosts that may or may not exist, or was it his kiss? More than likely it was from his question. She could run. That's what she'd always done. But it wouldn't work. She could never run far enough or fast enough to get away from her feelings for Brody.

Tired of questioning herself, and exhausted from the years of running, Hannah opted to take charge. She slid her leg across his until she straddled him and felt his hardness against her core. Holy man, he was gorgeous. And if everything he'd told her was true, he was hers.

Ghosts or no ghosts, there wasn't a chance in hell she would leave this desert tonight. Tonight belonged to them. The ghosts couldn't possess her soul because she was about to give it to Brody.

"Yes," she finally said. "I want you to be with me." Just saying it made her feel freer than she had ever been.

Brody nipped at her jaw, rocked his body against hers. "For how long?"

"Let's start with one night."

He kissed her hard, sweeping his tongue over hers again and again. Cradling her face, he gave her a scorching look. "One night will never be enough."

Truer words had never been spoken.

11

A STRANGE HAPPENING AT THE LAST CALL

J. Piper Lee

Kat scooped up her classwork from the bar and set it out of the way on her makeshift desk, away from the possibility of getting liquor on it.

Her profs were pretty understanding that she ran a business as well as being a part-time student, but papers smelling of bourbon were not going to get her any extra credit.

It was about a half hour until the bar opened, so she had to get ready. The rest of her assignments would have to wait until after she closed.

She was not only the proprietor, she was the bartender. Kat had a couple part-timers that waited on the tables, while she mixed and poured and took care of the bar.

And The Booth.

Not that it was a lot of work, because it was right next to end of the bar, and, to be quite honest, no one ever sat in The Booth... for more than ten or fifteen minutes.

Her regulars here in Carson City just avoided it. They claimed it was haunted.

Kat admitted she didn't care to sit there herself. The Booth felt cold, and... sad.

Visitors that came in, they'd sit there, because it was open, then usually look uncomfortable and take their drinks to the bar, or anywhere but there.

It didn't affect her bottom line, one empty booth. In fact, it had become a bit of an urban legend with the residents, and brought in some folks that had a choice in watering holes.

* * *

After cutting up citrus, stocking up olives, onions, and cherries into her convenient garnish station, she heard a knock on the door and let in Abby, her help for the night.

"Hey Abbs." Kat flipped the lock behind her. "How was your Calc exam?"

Abby gave her a thumbs-up. "Got a B. No complaints."

They'd met on the Western Nevada College campus a few months ago in an English class. Kat had been looking for another server when Abby mentioned needing a part-time gig.

It had worked out well. Abby was learning bartending so she could spell Kat, and Kat understood scheduling Abby around nights she needed to go to a study group or had a big exam coming.

Mostly in silence, they took down chairs and wiped down tables.

Abby was already in her *Last Call* shirt, but added a waist apron, filling the pockets with pens, order slips, and coasters.

Kat placed a tray of beer glasses into the fridge to chill, and then, satisfied they were ready, unlocked the door and turned the open sign on.

Her first regular would be there in a few minutes.

She set a roll of quarters on the jukebox and fed a few in, selecting some tunes until the patrons could start choosing.

* * *

About two hours in, the night took a sharp turn.

A guy she'd never seen before entered the bar. He glanced around and then headed to one of the only free tables in the room.

The Booth.

Kat almost cringed when he slid onto the leather bench seat.

She finished a tray of drinks for Abby, then stepped over and greeted her new customer.

"Evening. What can I get you?" She sat a cardboard coaster and napkin in front of him.

"Hi. Can I get an amber ale, in a glass, please?" he smiled.

Not affected by the haunted corner yet. "Sure."

Kat grabbed a glass from the rack, popped the top of a local microbrew she stocked in the requested style and poured it before heading back over with the glass and a bowl of pretzels. "Enjoy."

"Thanks."

* * *

She watched him, as unobtrusively as possible, all evening as he enjoyed the ale and just seemed to want to listen to the music and let the chatter wash over him.

He actually looked more relaxed as time progressed. It was very unsettling.

Around 10 p.m., he paid up, left a generous tip, and nodded to her on his way out.

* * *

Her new "regular" came pretty much five days a week, always after seven, sometimes later. Sat in The Booth, ordered two or three ales, ate some pretzels, and left by ten at the latest.

He stayed later on Friday nights, and had yet to come in on Saturday or Sunday.

After a few weeks, she was dying to know why he wasn't bothered by that seat, that booth. But how did she ask someone if they got the willies?

She decided to start up a little conversation one evening.

"How's your week?" Kat smiled as she delivered his drink.

He sighed, looking up at her. "Long."

Hot damn. This was the first time she'd really seen his eyes. They were Blue Eyes.

Very Blue Eyes.

Then he smiled.

"Can... can I get you anything else?" Jeez, did she just stammer?

He looked around at the sparse crowd. "Can you sit for a minute?"

Kat caught Mikey's eye and nodded at the bar. He moved over to stand behind the counter as she sat across from Very Blue Eyes.

162

He reached across the table. "Marcus Williams." He shrugged. "Marc."

"Kat Carrin." She grasped his hand, noting it was as nice as his everything else.

"Carrin. You're the owner?"

She was surprised he'd noticed the very subtle sign out front. *Katrine Carrin, Proprietor*

"And bartender, and cleaning staff with a side of procurement."

"Wow. And student based on the text books and backpack."

Kat grinned. "I'm finishing my last few classes."

He asked about her degree.

She told him, then got up to mix a few drinks that Mikey wasn't familiar with, then returned with a beer for herself.

"So, what about you? What brought you to Carson City? Professional gambler?" She really hoped not.

Marc laughed. "No, much more boring. I'm a doctor. I work at the medical center."

"You're a specialist, then?" There was only one medical center: Carson Tahoe Specialists.

"Yes. Ortho. That's why it was a long week. Ski season."

They talked for a while longer before Kat returned to tend bar. After which Marc asked her to join him for lunch the next day.

She had a project to finish, but she decided she could spare a couple hours.

They agreed to meet at Tito's at noon.

Maybe there, at a neutral location, she could see if he was different away from the effects of The Booth. Which hadn't felt as boothy tonight. She usually got the same creepies as everyone else sitting there.

But tonight, with Marc, it didn't seem as bad. We'll, he'd had an effect on her, maybe he was having an effect on her haunted bar.

* * *

Cat made herself get up a bit earlier than she usually would on a Saturday so she could get some studying done before she met Marc.

She'd likely pay for it that night, but it had been a long time since she'd been on a date–probably since she'd moved to Carson City.

She, like Marc, was not one of the many lifelong local residents.

"Tell me what brought you here." They were enjoying margaritas and chips while their food was being prepared.

"Actually, I was born here. My mom died when I was four and my dad moved us to Sacramento. He said for a job, but I think there were too many memories here for him. He never talked much about her or what happened."

Kat slipped her hand into his and gave it a comforting squeeze.

"My dad always put me off when I asked about her, so I let it go until he passed away from liver disease a couple years ago. I saw the opening at Carson while I was doing some digging on my mom, and it seemed like a sign to move back."

When he didn't elaborate, Kat picked up the conversation. "Small world. I was born in Sacramento. When I was in second grade, I think, we moved to Reno. My dad thought he was some great gambler, just because he got lucky when he was there one time. My mom worked as an accountant for one of the casinos. It kept food on the table and a roof over our heads."

"So not really a great gambler?"

"He could have been, but he never could stop when he was ahead. I left the minute I graduated high school and moved here. I got a job waiting tables at the bar. The old man that owned it liked me for some reason and taught me how to mix drinks and run the place. Rusty let me stay in the apartment on the second floor for free as long as I was taking classes. He left it to me when he died."

"You live over the bar?" Marc resisted when she made to pull her hand away.

His thumb gently stroked across her fingers.

"Yeah, it has everything I need and saves me a lot of money. I want to buy the building next door."

"Bigger bar?"

"Restaurant. There's a serious lack of places to eat around here."

The waiter arrived with a tray full of food, so they reluctantly let go and he served.

Once he was gone, they dug in. Kat had been to Tito's a million times, but this was Marc's first visit.

He admittedly had been mostly working and eating fast food or whatever things he knew how to cook.

"And what would those be?"

"Mac and cheese. Canned soup. I do make a hell of a grilled cheese." Marc's smile was wry. "But I may be coming here more often; this is fantastic. I'm not sure I ever had Mexican like this."

"This is Tex-Mex. Romero and his family came here from the Rio Grande Valley. It's not the more traditional Mexican we get here and in Cali." She was enjoying one of her favorites, fajita quesadillas. "But it's awesome."

* * *

Marc walked back with her to the bar. It was a bit brisker than when she walked over, but she tended to hoof it where she could, or take the bus to school. Her car was old, and she really needed to get a newer one.

But she had a plan, and that would set her back.

As they traversed the few blocks, Kat got the nerve to bring up The Booth.

"So, I've been meaning to ask you something–about your regular seat at the bar." How the hell did she put this?

"You mean the haunted booth?" He laughed.

"How did you know about that?" She stopped dead on the sidewalk. "Did you always know?"

Marc took her hand and pulled her until she started walking again. She noticed he kept ahold of her, and she didn't object.

"Bob's bum knee is under my care. We're trying to put off replacement surgery as long as we can. And well, he grilled me about sitting there."

Bob was a regular at Last Call.

Kat waited for Marc to elaborate. When he seemed content to just enjoy the walk, she couldn't contain herself. "So?"

"It's just a booth." He shrugged.

When they arrived, he asked if he could come in for a minute.

Once inside, Marc laid his coat on the bar and stood in front of his usual spot. Almost staring at the space.

Kat tossed hers next to his, resting her elbow on the wood surface, waiting to see what was on his mind.

"I meant it when I told Bob that I don't feel anything weird in the booth. But it's not just a booth. I came in that first time for a reason."

She suddenly had a very bad feeling–something Rusty had told her one night he'd been drinking a few more than he should have.

"Oh, my God."

Marc turned to face her. "You know the story then. Of what happened to Vera Moore."

"I only know what Rusty told me. I don't even know if it's true."

He pulled out his wallet and removed a folded sheet of paper. "Here's the police report. I haven't read it yet. Can you tell me what you've heard and then we can see if they agree? I just don't want to read it off a piece of paper."

Kat nodded slipping onto the bar stool behind her and gesturing for Marc sit next to her. "Please."

He did, but faced the bar, his eyes locked on the scarred surface.

She took his hand in hers, locking their fingers together. "Rusty used to get a little soused on the day his wife passed. She had cancer and died about ten years before he did. One year after the bar closed, he sat right about here and was just staring at the corner. He started talking about one night a couple came in and sat there. They were arguing on and off. Rusty said he never heard what they were fighting about. He'd gone to get a case of beer when he heard a gunshot. When he ran out, the man was gone. He called 911 and tried to help her. She died at the hospital and her husband was never found."

Marc's grip on her hand was almost painfully tight, but he needed an anchor right now. She'd missed it before, when he looked so comfortable in The Booth… the fine tension in his body. It was always there, hidden behind his easy smile.

She picked up the police report and scanned it. It verified most of what Rusty told her. "It says Matthew Moore was never apprehended and was assumed to have fled the area with his four-year-old son, Jason."

"I don't know how he managed to change our names. I have a pretty legitimate looking birth certificate. Marcus Jason Williams." He made a scoffing noise. "He wasn't a particularly loving dad, but he wasn't abusive or anything. I guess I should just be lucky he didn't shoot me too."

Kat brought their joined hands and pressed them to her cheek. "I'm so sorry."

He finally turned and looked at her. There were tears in his eyes. "I guess I should tell them that he's dead."

"I think that can probably wait." Kat felt helpless.

And she hadn't in a long time, not since she moved here and started making decisions for herself. She reached over and was about to grab a handful of napkins for him when he pulled a handkerchief out of his back pocket.

Then he handed it to her. She hadn't even realized she was also tearing up.

Damn, she really liked this guy. But he had an airport full of baggage, and she was not without her own.

She hadn't liked a guy in a long time. And she liked Marcus. A lot.

They sat there for a time, in silence.

* * *

Abby arrived for her shift, looking surprised that someone was there with Kat. When Kat mentioned they'd gone to lunch and were talking, Abby gave her thumbs-up behind Marc's back.

He had said his goodbyes after Kat had initiated a long hard hug. "I'll call you tomorrow, if that's okay?"

"I'd like that." Kat walked him out and started the usual prep for the evening.

"Boss!" Abby called out from across the room. "Spill."

Kat forced a chuckle. "We had lunch. That was it." Marc's history was his and his alone.

* * *

Marc did call the next day. Told her he'd stopped at the police station and talked to the detective that got him the case file. They confirmed that the husband was Marc's dad. The detective said he'd request a death certificate from Sac PD and close the file. He also offered to check into how the name change didn't come across the active warrant on his dad.

Kat told him that Vera was buried just down the way from the bar in Lone Mountain Cemetery. She was about to ask him if he wanted to go visit the grave when his pager went off.

"Emergency at the hospital, I gotta go."

"Drive careful, the snow's really starting to come down." Kat flopped back on her bed where she'd been practicing for her final presentation.

It was a chunk of her grade in this class and she wanted to know it by rote, like how she knew how to make a Lemon Drop without cracking open a cocktail book.

Lemon juice, sugar, citron vodka, Cointreau, simple syrup topped with a wedge.

It was her comfort zone, behind the bar, but she wanted to get her degree and expand her business. Not ever have to worry about a place to sleep or food or relying on anyone other than herself.

That didn't preclude her from wanting to get to know Marc better. She never wanted to be wholly reliant on someone just because she loved them; she'd seen that dysfunction with her mom.

She was fairly confident she could love "Very Blue Eyes and Carries a Handkerchief" and remain herself.

They'd just have to carry their own baggage until they got rid of it.

* * *

They started spending more time together in the next weeks. Lunches at Tito's, cafeteria trays at the hospital in between her classes. One night, he made her mac and cheese... with soup.

Sometimes when it was slow, she sat across from him in the booth and did classwork while they talked.

It wasn't The Booth anymore.

The malaise that had permeated it was gone. Maybe Vera was content that her son knew the truth, maybe that anyone knew the truth. They would probably never know.

My son is happy. So I am happy.

Kat's head popped up.

Marc was scrolling through Twitter or something but looked up when she started.

"What?" His brow furrowed in concern.

Kat shook her head, her eyes sliding over the small metal plaque on the wall.

In Memory of Vera Moore.

"Just remembered something." She stretched out her feet until they were tangled with his. She looked at the way he was slouched across from her, relaxed. The tension was gone.

A large group had come in the door. Break time was over. Kat stacked her notebooks and papers.

"Hey, are you gonna stay over?"

"Planning on it." Marc leaned forward as she rose and stretched across the table for a kiss.

It had been the easiest thing in her life, falling in love with this man.

After all the hard they'd both endured, it felt right.

He makes me happy too, Vera.

Kat grinned at Marc as she slipped out of the booth and got back to work.

13Thirty Books

Exciting Thrillers, Heart-Warming Romance,
Mind-Bending Horror, Sci-Fantasy
and
Educational Non-Fiction

The Third Hour

The Third Hour is an original spin on the religious-thriller genre, incorporating elements of science fiction along with the religious angle. Its strength lies in this originality, combined with an interesting take on real historical figures, who are made a part of the experiment at the heart of the novel, and the fast pace that builds.

Ripper – A Love Story

"Queen Victoria would not be amused—but you will be by this beguiling combination of romance and murder. Is the Crown Prince of England really Jack the Ripper? His wife would certainly like to know… and so will you."
Diana Gabaldon, New York Times Best Selling Author

Heather Graham's Haunted Treasures

Presented together for the first time, New York Times Bestselling Author, Heather Graham brings back three tales of paranormal love and adventure.

Heather Graham's Christmas Treasures

New York Times Bestselling Author, Heather Graham brings back three out-of-print Christmas classics that are sure to inspire, amaze, and warm your heart.

Zodiac Lovers Series

Zodiac Lovers is a series of romantic, gay, paranormal novelettes. In each story, one of the lovers has all the traits of his respective zodiacal sign.

Never Fear

Shh… Something's Coming

Never Fear – Phobias

Everyone Fears Something

Never Fear – Christmas Terrors

He sees you when you're sleeping …

More Than Magick

Why me? Recent college grad Scott Madison, has been recruited (for reasons that he will eventually understand) by the wizard Arion and secretly groomed by his ostensible friend and mentor, Jake Kesten. But his training hasn't readied him to face Vraasz, a being who has become powerful enough to destroy the universe and whose first objective is the obliteration of Arion's home world. Scott doesn't understand why he was the chosen one or why he is traveling the universe with a ragtag group of individuals also chosen by Arion. With time running out, Scott discovers that he has a power that can defeat Vraasz. If only he can figure out how to use it.

Stop Saying Yes – Negotiate!

Stop Saying Yes - Negotiate! is the perfect "on the go" guide for all negotiations. This easy-to-read, practical guide will enable you to quickly identify the other side's tactics and strategies allowing you to defend yourself ensuring a better negotiation for your side and theirs.

13Thirtybooks.com
facebook.com/13thirty

Made in the USA
Columbia, SC
08 May 2018